THE MASTER OF BARRACUDA ISLE

THE MASTER OF BARRACUDA ISLE

It was with the best and kindest of intentions that Jan was here on Barracuda Island, off Australia's Great Barrier Reef, posing as her sister Felicity. She wanted to help Felicity and her boyfriend Jarvis against opposition to their marriage from Jarvis's guardian, his arrogant, intolerant uncle Ludovic Fairlie, who decreed Jarvis was too young to marry. Although at first Jan told herself she hated Ludovic, it was not long before she was feeling rather differently, so what could she do, now that he had apparently changed his mind and was making enthusiastic plans for her marriage to his nephew?

The Master Of Barracuda Isle

by

Hilary Wilde

Dales Large Print Books
Long Preston, North Yorkshire,
BD23 4ND, England.

British Library Cataloguing in Publication Data.

Wilde, Hilary
    The master of Barracuda Isle.

    A catalogue record of this book is
    available from the British Library

    ISBN   978-1-84262-690-0 pbk

First published in Great Britain in 1971
by Mills & Boon Limited

Cover illustration © Gordon Crabb by arrangement with
Alison Eldred

The moral right of the author has been asserted

Published in Large Print 2009 by arrangement with
The Estate of the late Mrs Clare Breton Smith,
care of Juliet Burton Literary Agency

679858

Dales Large Print is an imprint of Library Magna Books Ltd.

F

Printed and bound in Great Britain by
T.J. (International) Ltd., Cornwall, PL28 8RW

CHAPTER ONE

The front door bell rang impatiently, but Jan, washing her hair, decided to ignore it, for none of the friends she and Felicity, her sister, had made during their six months in Australia would visit them at nine a.m., nor did she feel in the mood to cope with salesmen.

That morning she had overslept, waking in the quiet flat, for Iris, who now shared it with her, had long left for work. Jan had faced the fact that this was going to be just another typical day, dragging on endlessly, while she fought her unhappiness. She had looked through the newspaper as she drank her coffee and there were many advertisements for new jobs, but not what she wanted. It had to be one at least a thousand miles away from Sydney and the man she still loved, so she tossed the paper to the floor, then had a cool shower, for the morning was already hot. She had nothing to do, so had washed her hair, and now the front door bell was ringing!

It went on ringing and ringing, as if whoever was pressing the button was determined to get an answer.

Sighing, she grabbed a green towel, twisting her long ebony-black hair under it, then pulled on her green towelling coat, tightening the belt.

'I'm coming!' she shouted as the bell went on shrilly, and she made her way through the pages of the newspaper, strewn over the floor, and paper patterns and materials that were falling off the divan where Iris slept. It looked a mess all right, Jan thought, and wondered what her mother, over ten thousand miles away, would say if she could see it.

At last Jan reached the door and opened it. On the narrow landing stood a tall, broad-shouldered man. He looked like a typical Australian at first sight, with his rugged face, sun-tanned skin and bleached blond hair, yet there was something different about him.

'Miss Shaw?' His voice was curt. 'Miss Janet Shaw?'

'Yes,' she snapped back. Who did he think he was, anyway, she thought, for he had a nerve, ringing the bell like that. Why, she might have been ill... 'What do you want?'

Her anger made her unhappy dark eyes brighten, brought colour to her high cheek-bones as she lifted her pointed chin and glared at him.

'May I come in?' he asked. It was more like a statement, even a command, than a request, she thought. Now she knew what was *different* about him. He was the kind of arrogant man she loathed.

As she saw his eyebrows lift and he looked amused, she was convinced she had seen him before, somewhere, but now, holding the door firmly and refusing to recognise the truth that if he was determined to enter her flat she would find it impossible to stop him, she said:

'Who are you?'

He looked even more amused, as if something she had said was funny.

'Ludovic Fairlie,' he told her.

She frowned, for the name was vaguely familiar. He seemed to be waiting as if expecting an immediate reaction, she thought as she stared at the broad-shouldered man in an elegantly-cut grey suit. She wondered if she ought to know the name.

'What do you want?' she insisted, still wary.

He smiled. She had a real shock, for it had

the strangest effect on his face, wiping out the aloof sternness and the arrogance she disliked. He even laughed.

'How right you are to be cautious. I'm Jarvis Fairlie's uncle.'

'Oh, Jarvis!'

Her hand flew to her mouth as she stared up at the man. Now she knew who he was. He was not only the uncle of Felicity's boyfriend, Jarvis, but he was famous as one of the wealthiest men in Sydney, a business tycoon. His photograph was always in the local papers, showing him on his yacht, or with his latest racing car, or else escorting some of the world's most beautiful girls, for he was definitely one of the jet-set when he wanted to be. He was renowned for his dedication to his work, his impatience with weaklings, his insistence on perfection.

Jarvis, his nephew, was still at university, more interested in having a good time than working hard, which was one way in which he and his uncle didn't see eye to eye. Jarvis was always grumbling about his uncle's meanness, lectures, and threats to reduce Jarvis's allowance. Jarvis also resented bitterly the will of his grandfather which had made Jarvis Ludovic's ward, and which also meant Jarvis could not touch his inheritance until he was twenty-five.

'Of course…' Jan said, standing back and opening the door, 'please come in,' she added, wondering what on earth Jarvis's uncle could want with her. Had he heard about Felicity, perhaps, and disapproved of the romance? 'I'm sorry it's all such a mess,' Jan apologised as they went into the small gloomy room with its aged armchairs, and the divan bed against the wall, where Iris slept, and which was covered by a bright red and black knitted cover, and remnants of Iris's dressmaking activities. It really did look pretty ghastly, Jan thought. If she'd only known Jarvis's uncle was calling!

He was looking round with a rather supercilious smile.

'You live here alone.'

'No, with a friend. She's at work. Please sit down,' said Jan, nearly tripping in her bare feet over a hole in the faded red carpet. She felt suddenly embarrassed, aware of the disapproval in his eyes as he looked round the untidy shabby room. Then a wave of anger swept through her, for after all, what right had he to judge her? He was a wealthy man who thought in thousands of dollars, whereas she and Felicity had come out to Australia, on a working holiday and to discover if Jarvis and Felicity were really in love, and had to watch every cent they spent.

Jerking back the pale pink curtains that were still half-pulled across the only window – and seeing with dismay how badly the curtains needed washing – Jan saw the pathetic souvenir of her love affair with George. Just the sight of it hurt her – the solitary, rather jaded-looking red carnation, last remnant of the flowers he had given her before his diplomatic brush-off. Now, suddenly, she wanted to cry.

'May I sit down?'

Ludovic's ultra-patient voice jerked Jan back to the present.

'I'm sorry,' she apologised sincerely, feeling her cheeks burn. 'I was thinking.'

'I can see that,' he said, sounding amused, as he looked carefully at the two armchairs, both shabby and rather pathetic, before he sat down. He glanced at the pages of the newspaper scattered on the carpet, one of them showing some exciting pictures of Surfers' Paradise and of the Snowy Mountains.

'Planning a holiday?' he asked casually.

'Yes,' she said quickly. It wasn't the truth, but she didn't feel inclined to tell him why she was looking for a remote part of Australia in which to get a job. She could imagine how Ludovic Fairlie would smile, that condescending smile of his, and probably tell her that she would get over it and that it was cowardly and non-constructive to run away.

He smiled at her and again she had that feeling of confusion, for he looked so different, younger, much nicer, when he smiled. His whole face seemed to relax, losing its hard arrogant look. It also revived her certainty that they had met before somewhere. Or if they hadn't actually met, she must have seen him in person.

Without thinking, she asked:

'*Have* we met somewhere?'

His thick fair eyebrows lifted.

'If we had, I'm sure I'd have remembered,' he said.

She felt her cheeks burn.

'I've probably seen your picture in the papers.'

'Probably. But to go back to this holiday question, it's rather interesting because, you see, I've come with an invitation. Jarvis's mother is eager to meet you.'

He handed her an envelope. It was sealed. She was so surprised, for why should Jarvis's

15

mother want to meet *her?* that her fingers seemed all thumbs and she had difficulty in opening the envelope, being very conscious of the amusement in Ludovic Fairlie's eyes all the time.

But at last she had it open and read the brief typed letter.

'Dear Miss Shaw,

I would be delighted if you paid me a visit. I like to meet Jarvis's friends, so do hope you can accept my invitation.'

It was signed Agnes Fairlie in a flowery, almost dramatic writing.

'But why...' Jan began. She was puzzled, for Jarvis was Felicity's boy-friend, not hers.

Ludovic sighed.

'Miss Shaw, I wonder if you'd mind sitting down and also would you remove that ghastly towel from your head? At any moment it's going to fall and it's getting on my nerves!'

Jan obeyed, almost falling into the other armchair and jumping as she sat on one of the broken springs. Then she pulled off the towel, letting her wet hair, ebony-black and waist-length, fall in a cloud, brushing it back from her face with an impatient movement.

'I'm sorry,' she said, stiff with anger, 'I overslept this morning, and was washing my

16

hair. We don't usually get visitors at this hour.'

'I tried to phone, but my secretary couldn't find your number,' he said coldly.

'We're not in the directory yet.'

Much to her annoyance, Jan was feeling uncomfortably aware that she must look rather odd, for her towelling coat was too short, showing off her long legs. Normally this would not worry her, but there was something about this man that made her hate giving him the chance to look disapprovingly at her. For that was the kind he was – smug, domineering, arrogant, impossible, she decided. How she hated that type of man! For that matter, she admitted to herself, she hated all men. You just could not trust them.

'Jarvis didn't tell you I was coming to see you?' Ludovic Fairlie asked, his voice stern.

'No, but … but…' She was about to say she hadn't seen Jarvis for some time, but Ludovic went on talking.

'I told him to. Will he never grow up?'

'He's only twenty and probably swotting hard for his exams…' Jan leapt to Jarvis's defence immediately.

'And how old are you?' Ludovic asked.

'Nineteen,' she replied without thinking,

and then was annoyed with herself, for it was a stupid question and she need not have answered it. 'Why?'

'Why?' he smiled. 'I just wondered. You look so absurdly young.'

The patronage in his voice was too much for Jan.

'I suppose we all do to old people,' she snapped, and then was sorry; it was a childish remark. He merely smiled.

'Yes, I suppose to you and Jarvis I am a square oldie. Funny that today you're supposed to have had it by the time you're thirty-three,' he laughed. 'The truth is, and this is what you kids don't understand, that a man in his thirties is in his prime. This is the most exciting...'

George had been thirty-three too, Jan was remembering. That had been one of his excuses. The difference in their ages, the fact that he disliked marriage and its responsibilities, his ambitions for his future, all words he said to hide the simple truth: that he did not love her, nor ever had!

'Miss Shaw,' Ludovic's angry voice penetrated her thoughts, 'you're not listening to a word I'm saying.'

He was right. She looked at him.

'I'm sorry,' she said, and meant it. 'I didn't

18

mean to be rude, I was thinking…'

'Obviously.'

She looked away, her eyes suddenly smarting.

'I'm rather upset and…'

'I'm not surprised,' he said coldly.

Startled, she turned round to stare at him enquiringly and Ludovic went on slowly:

'After all, marriage to a man you hardly know and who is still at college is a big step to take.'

Her mouth was dry. He'd got everything wrong. George was thirty-three, certainly not at college, for he had a very good job at a stockbrokers. In any case, how could Ludovic Fairlie know anything about George?

Ludovic continued:

'Naturally Jarvis's mother is troubled. She feels he should complete his education and be settled in a job before thinking of matrimony. However, she was impressed by the letters he wrote to her. He seems very much in love…' Ludovic's mouth twisted as if he was trying not to smile, 'and that's why she would like to meet you and see if you…'

Make the grade. Jan finished the sentence silently for him. For a moment she could not speak, and hardly think, she was so confused. How could Jarvis's mother think he was in love with her when it was Felicity...

'But Jarvis doesn't...' she began, then stopped; she had thought of something.

Had Jarvis deliberately given them the wrong impression? After all, Felicity was even younger than she was, only seventeen, and so many people were snobs, perhaps Jarvis's mother didn't approve of him marrying a dancer. Had Jarvis deliberately–? She began to wonder, then Ludovic interrupted.

'You were saying, "but Jarvis doesn't..."'

Jan thought fast and said:

'He doesn't want to get married yet. He does realise his exams are important and...'

'Does he? His mother got the impression that he wanted to get married right away.'

Ludovic's voice was icily cold with disapproval now, almost as if he blamed Jan for Jarvis's 'idiocy'.

Not sure what to say, finding herself wondering if Jarvis had invented it all for some reason and not wanting to let him down, Jan jumped up, forgetting for a moment her bare feet she had carefully tucked under her, and her long bare legs.

'Can I make you a cup of coffee? I'll just get dressed. It won't take a moment and...'

But he had stood up, too. Gone were the smiles and now his face was unfriendly.

'Please don't bother, Miss Shaw. I take it you'll accept my sister-in-law's invitation? I'll call for you at ten o'clock tomorrow morning. Please be punctual.'

He walked to the door and turned. Jan, feeling almost frozen with shock as she tried to work out what she should say or do, stared at him. Would she be helping Jarvis, who had been kind to her, by going to meet his mother?

'Miss Shaw, where my sister-in-law lives it's very hot indeed. I would suggest you bring your lightest frocks and, of course, your swimming gear. Goodbye.'

He gave her a long searching look, then opened the door, closing it behind him. Jan stood still for a moment, completely unaware of how lovely she looked, the pale green towelling intensifying the colour of her long black hair and clear skin. When she could move, she collapsed in the chair, not sure if she wanted to cry or laugh. Ludovic Fairlie certainly was a character! The way he issued orders and took it for granted you would do everything he demanded! she thought. He was impossible, typical of everything she hated in men.

She wondered what he had thought of her, looking the mess she did, living in a scruffy horrible little flat which it was, but it was the best they could afford.

Jan could imagine him talking to his sister-in-law. 'Not quite the *right* wife for Jarvis.' Jan pretended she was Ludovic and spoke in his arrogant voice. 'Not at all suitable, I'm afraid.'

Going to the phone, Jan tried to get Jarvis without success; not that she had much hope, for he was sure to be at some lecture, so she decided to phone later.

She dressed, slipped out of the flat to shop for their evening meal and hurried back, tidying up, trying to make the flat look better than it must have done to Ludovic Fairlie.

Somehow she kept seeing him in her mind and each time she felt certain she *had* seen him before, not only in the newspapers but in real life.

The long day finally dragged out and Iris who shared the flat came home from work.

'How smart the flat is,' she teased as she came in, a short plump girl with blue eyes that matched her dress. 'Did you feel like spring-cleaning?'

They had met in a discotheque shortly

after Felicity had gone to Cairns, with the company, to dance. Jan had been lonely, and, since she had left her job because of George, was rather hard up, so as Iris wanted somewhere to live it had seemed a perfect solution to share the flat. Iris would move in, but move out when Felicity returned, Iris had promised.

Over their meal of grilled fish, Iris listened as Jan told her about the day.

'Not *the* Ludovic Fairlie,' said Iris, her voice awed, her plump body tightly encased in the blue jeans and white shirt she always wore at home. 'My, Jan, you really are going places. I didn't realise Jarvis was his nephew.'

'Yes, but they don't get on well.'

'We've known one another such a short time,' Iris said. 'I've often wondered what made you and your sister come out here.'

Jan laughed, helping herself to more chipped potatoes.

'Love ... just love,' she joked, then half-closed her eyes, for the words still hurt. 'Jarvis came over to England for a year to the university near us and he met Felicity. They fell in love and when Jarvis came back he asked Felicity to come out. My mother – she's a widow and runs a boutique – wasn't

23

very keen on the idea, as Felicity wasn't seventeen then, so Mum suggested I came with my sister and we had a working holiday out here to give Felicity a chance to see if she really did love Jarvis.'

'She must miss you both,' Iris said, collecting the plates, talking over her shoulder as she got out the fruit salad Jan had left in the tiny fridge. 'Your mum, I mean!'

'She does. I write often. In a way, it was to help me, too,' Jan said, twisting a fork slowly on the table, avoiding Iris's eyes. 'You'll laugh at this, but my heart had been broken.'

'That makes it twice,' said Iris. 'Time you learned.'

'Don't worry,' said Jan. 'I'm never going to fall in love again. I hate men – especially men like Ludovic Fairlie.'

'I wouldn't mind him,' Iris mused thoughtfully. 'All that lovely lolly!'

'Money isn't everything, Iris. Well, you see there was Frank. I grew up with him, so to speak. He lived next door and his mother was an invalid and he was always with us and ... well, it was just one of those things. I took it for granted we would marry, have children and live happily ever after, and then I found I didn't love him and then...'

'Then...?' Iris sat down at the table, pushing Jan's fruit salad towards her.

'Then he agreed and told me that it was all childish nonsense, that I saw him as a myth.'

'A myth?'

'He said I'd built up a dream-man image and made him fit it, and he wasn't my dream man.'

'So?'

'So it was all over. Even though I was unsure, I felt absolutely shattered, because he didn't love me. You see I'd gone everywhere with him. Felicity always had boyfriends, she's terribly pretty, but I always had Frank, so I never needed a boy-friend. Mum thought it would do me good too, to come out here, and...'

'You met George? Go on while I wash up,' said Iris, gathering the plates.

'Well, you know all that. I met George and was lost.' Jan sighed. 'I must have been frightfully naïve to think he loved me.'

'He put on a very good act from what you said,' Iris pointed out. 'He sounds an absolute heel to me. I bet you he'll marry a stockbroker's daughter.'

'He did say if ever he married, it would be for a material reason.' Jan glanced at the clock. 'I must phone Jarvis. I've got to know

25

what he's been up to, you…'

She went to the phone and tried to get him, again without success. She turned to Iris, who was now kneeling on the ground, carefully pinning the pieces of a pattern to a wide strip of yellow and green silk.

'What shall I do?' Jan asked worriedly. 'If I'm to help Jarvis, I must know what he's told his mother about me.'

Iris sat back on her heels.

'You think he's pretending it's *you* because he doesn't think they'll approve of Felicity?'

'I don't know what to think,' Jan tossed back her long dark hair, 'but I must know what he's up to. Jarvis, I mean.'

'Tell you what,' Iris jumped to her feet. 'Let's try the Brown Owl. Lots of the students go there.'

'That's a good idea. Jarvis has taken me there for coffee.'

'I thought Jarvis was your *sister's* boy-friend?' Iris teased, standing before the mirror, combing her short blonde hair.

'He was… I mean, is. They were sorry for me about George, and Jarvis and Felicity took me to a ball at the University once, with a blind date, of course. I didn't like him, but then…'

'You don't like men,' Iris finished for her.

'At the moment,' she added.

Jan smiled.

'Well, after Felicity went north, Jarvis went on seeing me. I think he was sorry for me. We had coffee out and dinner once, but lately I haven't seen him. He was just kind and that was all,' she finished.

They went down the two flights of stairs to the front door of the terraced house, then out into the humid heat of the Australian evening. They walked along the brightly lit streets of Kings Cross, rubbing shoulders with people of every nationality, hearing every language that could be spoken, pausing, as Jan always did, to admire the gorgeous brilliance of the fountain, and then following their favourite pastime, shop-gazing. Finally they reached the coffee house.

The room was packed, but Jan and Iris managed to squeeze their way through between chairs and tables and finally found Nick Peters, a friend of Jarvis.

'Hi, Jan, good to see you.' Nick, a tall thin student, stood up. 'You want Jarvis? He's in custody.'

Jan looked up sharply, then saw the laughter in Nick's eyes.

'He's dining with his uncle,' Nick went on with a grin. 'That's custody all right!'

27

'Nick, if you see him, would you ask him to phone me at once?' She saw the amused question in his eyes and didn't smile back. 'I mean it, Nick – it's something to do with his uncle. He came to see me and...'

'Whew!' Nick whistled. 'Poor you! Proper monster, isn't he? And stuffy. I wonder if he was ever young... Okay, I'll tell Jarvis, but I'm not sure I'll see him until the lectures tomorrow.'

'Please try, Nick. I'll be in until ten tomorrow morning and after that...' Some girls in gaily coloured clothes came crowding round the table.

'Nick,' a pretty young blonde girl with long hair hanging down her back said reproachfully, 'you promised...'

Jan stared at the group of girls, all in their mid-teens, and suddenly she felt absurdly old.

'Thanks, Nick,' she said, and escaped.

Iris was waiting for her.

'No luck?'

'No. Jarvis is dining with his uncle. I only wish I knew what Jarvis was at.'

Back in the flat, while Iris was cutting out the new dress she was making, Jan wrote to Jarvis.

'I hadn't understood at first, but now I

realise you want me to stand in for Felicity, so I played along, though I do feel rather bad about it, but you were so kind to me. Well, I'll be only too glad to help. But please don't pile it on or it might get awkward, as already they seem to think we're planning an immediate wedding. Anyhow, I'll get to know your mother and it might help things for you when Felicity gets back. I'm sure they'll feel she's too young for marriage, but we'll hope for the best. By the way, in case you haven't heard from Felicity, her tour has been extended for another month. I know you'll be disappointed, but she says it means a rise in salary and perhaps a chance to be on T.V., and she's thrilled.'

Jan's next letter was to her mother. This was tricky, for Jan had been careful to say nothing about their trouble in finding a flat they could afford, or her unhappiness. She had never mentioned George, as she thought her mother would say she'd been caught on the rebound, that grieving for Frank had made her fall in love with George, and Jan had felt in no mood for a lecture no matter how loving it was. So each letter, now, was difficult to write as she mustn't let her mother have any idea about the void in her life. Jan wrote that she had been thinking of changing her job in order to see more of Australia and that she had been invited by Jarvis's mother to stay with her.

'Felicity is up in Cairns, dancing, and Jarvis studying hard, so it seems a good idea. It'll be fun to have a holiday.'

Jan also wrote to Felicity.

'I know it all sounds crazy, because as I thought at once, why did Jarvis's mother want to see *me*. It's you she should see, as he loves *you!*'

Felicity, Jan was thinking as she wrote, could be easily and very jealous!

'I think it's some plan of Jarvis's to keep his uncle from knowing that it's you he loves, because Ludovic Fairlie would immediately say you were much too young. He's quite impossible, one of those arrogant, stuffy, pompous creatures who think they know everything. Anyhow I'll keep in touch and let you know what Jarvis's mother is like.'

Afterwards Jan and Iris went through Jan's wardrobe. She had bought quite a few dripdry dresses since coming out to Australia and she'd need those, she knew. The choice of her swimming gear was dicey. Finally she took two bikinis, one a sombre black, the other a vivid yellow, and she added a more demure one-piece costume in case Jarvis's mother was a square.

'I don't want to offend her,' Jan told Iris, who nodded understandingly.

That night Jan slept well. It was a pleasant change from the long nights of tossing and turning, trying not to cry, going over – word for word – the conversations she had had with George, to find out what had really gone wrong.

Iris woke her up to say goodbye.

'Have fun!'

Jan laughed. She felt suddenly light-hearted, looking forward to the holiday ahead.

'I'm wondering where they live. I forgot to ask.'

'I should think *anywhere* is the only answer,' Iris said, as she gulped down the coffee that was her breakfast. 'They've houses all over the place. Maybe it'll be on his yacht... Gee, Jan, I envy you.'

'Can you manage on your own here?' Jan asked, suddenly worried. 'I'm thinking of the rent. I shouldn't be away long, though. A few days, perhaps, at the most a week.'

Irish laughed.

'I can manage easily, thanks. I've just had

a rise, I forgot to tell you.'

She had a good job where she was indispensable as a receptionist, being able to talk several languages, and she was appreciated by her employers.

After Iris had gone, Jan rummaged around, found stamps and slipped out to post the letters, then hurried back, afraid the phone might ring while she was out. She sat by it, hopefully waiting for Jarvis to ring, for she needed briefing as to what he had said about his 'girl-friend'.

But the phone didn't ring and at ten o'clock to the second the front door bell rang. It must be Ludovic Fairlie, she thought, as she grabbed her red raincoat and her suitcase, before answering the door.

A chauffeur in neat olive green uniform was on the landing. 'Miss Shaw?' he asked, his voice impersonal but polite.

She nodded and his blank sun-tanned face creased momentarily into a smile.

'May I take your case?' he asked, and took it from her, leading the way to the steep narrow staircase and down to the ground floor.

An enormous white Rolls-Royce was waiting for them. The chauffeur opened the door, and sitting back, she looked on either side of her, feeling like a V.I.P. and wanting to giggle, wishing she had Iris with her to share the joke.

The driver drove swiftly but well, manoeuvring neatly the hazards of busy Sydney's crazy traffic. Finally the big white Rolls reached the airport. Surprise number one, Jan thought, as she looked with amazement round her, for somehow she hadn't expected to fly, although she knew that Australians were used to their enormous country, and thought nothing of flying anywhere, even if only for a few days.

'The master asked me to apologise for not being able to travel with you, Miss Shaw,' the chauffeur said stiffly, holding out an envelope. 'Your ticket is here and you'll be met. I will take your luggage for you. This way, please...'

Jan followed him through the glaring sunshine that seemed to penetrate her dark glasses. Already her thin, amber-coloured silk suit felt uncomfortably wet and the perspiration was bursting out in tiny bubbles on her face. At least, she comforted herself, there would be air-conditioning on the plane. Glancing at the ticket, she didn't recognise the name of her destination. Australian names could be so strange, yet fascinatingly so, like Wahronga … which, if sung rather sadly, sounded very beautiful. At the crowded airport the chauffeur moved with accustomed precision, obviously used to it, and soon Jan found herself seated in the plane.

Once airborne she looked around. The elderly man sitting next to her was reading a book upside down as his head nodded, so she was not tempted to talk to him, although she longed to find out where they were flying to.

It sounded too crazy to ask the pretty blonde air hostess: 'Where am I going?' They'd think she was mad – or being funny. Suddenly she wondered if she was doing a stupid thing. She felt unsure for could this be a trap? Yet where was the sense in that? She had no wealthy parents to have a ransom demanded of them. Yet how could she be sure Ludovic … or rather the man who *said* he was Ludovic Fairlie … yet how could she be sure he really was? Should she have asked to see his credentials? she wondered, and then had to smile at the thought of Ludovic's face had she done so.

After all, she reminded herself, Jarvis *had* been dining with his uncle the night before, so surely that linked up? Wouldn't it be a strange coincidence if he was with his uncle the same day that a stranger pretended to be Ludovic Fairlie?

For a moment she felt horribly alone. She thought of Lewes, with her mother baking their favourite scones for tea, and Frank racing round the garden, always close to Jan, there when she needed him, life as it had been in the past when she had felt so secure. But now…?

Yet there was nothing she could do, so she closed her eyes and finally fell asleep.

Jan awoke with a start as the impersonal voice came over the tannoy, asking them to tighten their seat belts, saying there might be a few bounces in the air as there was a lot of cloud about but that there was no cause for worry. The elderly man by Jan's side collected his things, smiled at her as they tightened their belts.

'Not scared?'

She smiled back. 'No. I'm used to flying.' She had had a good job in England as a shorthand-typist and had often flown to the Continent for holidays.

There was noise and bustle, the hostess hurrying up and down the aisle, making sure everything was all right, people laughing and talking, and Jan wondered how she could have been so foolish as to let herself worry about this trip. She was even amused at her own melodrama.

Ludovic Fairlie had invited her to visit his sister-in-law ... or rather, the sister-in-law, Jarvis's mother, had invited Jan. It was kind of them. There had been no pressure. She could have said No, if she had wanted to. It seemed strange somehow that a busy man like Ludovic Fairlie should have bothered to call and invite her himself. He could have posted the letter or sent his secretary, Jan was thinking, as the plane made a perfect landing. It looked as if Ludovic and Jarvis's mother were really worried about Jarvis and concerned for him, yet Jarvis rarely spoke of his mother and when he spoke of his uncle it was with impatience and annoyance. Certainly Jan knew her gratitude to Jarvis for his kindness and understanding might have influenced her, but this was balanced by her urgent need to get away from Sydney, so that the invitation had been welcome, almost the answer to her prayer.

Feeling much happier, she went down the steps into the glaring heat, and walked through the blazing sun across the tarmac to the huge group of modern buildings with the glass they seemed to be composed of, glittering in the sun.

She walked alone, the amber colour of her suit emphasising the ebony black beauty of her hair which was loosely tied back with a yellow bow. She looked round her curiously, wondering where they were. It had not been a very long flight, but distances in Australia still amazed her.

As she collected her luggage a man came to her side. He was tall, with a leathery tanned face, very blue eyes and bleached hair. He was wearing khaki shorts and shirt, the collar open.

'Miss Shaw?' he asked politely. When she nodded, he added: 'The master asked me to apologise, but he's been detained in Sydney. He'll be joining you as soon as possible. Please come this way.'

Puzzled, for in the beginning there had been no mention of Ludovic Fairlie accompanying her on the trip or spending the 'holiday' with her, Jan followed him. The invitation had been from Mrs Fairlie, Jarvis's mother, and had nothing to do with Ludovic, she thought. Was he so alarmed about Jarvis's future that he planned to help Jarvis's mother 'talk' to Jarvis's girl-friend? Jan wondered.

The sun-tanned man led the way to a car – not a white Rolls-Royce this time, Jan noticed with amusement, but an equally fabulous sort of car; a green Bentley. As he put the suitcase in the boot and opened the car door for her, the unknown man gave her a brief smile.

'I'm Barry Ryder, Miss Shaw, known as the master's right hand. Up here, that is. I hope you'll enjoy your stay on the Barrier Reef.'

Barrier Reef! Jan thought. Why, the very words spelled a sort of magic, for she had often heard how beautiful it was and had hoped to see it one day.

'I'm sure I will, Mr Ryder,' she said with a quick smile as he slid behind the steering wheel of the car, and she sat back, looking round her curiously.

He grinned. 'Barry is the name, Miss Shaw.'

As the car carried them along, Jan glanced everywhere, delighting in it all, the clearness of the air, the pale blue sky that was incredibly cloudless, the flowers in the gardens which were all such exotic wonderful colours of red, yellow, white, even blue and purple, and then above all the beauty of the palm trees. It all fascinated her, and soon they had left most of the traffic behind, driving quickly through a town and then along a straight long road that seemed to stretch for ever ahead.

Jan closed her eyes drowsily and woke up when the car stopped.

Surprise number two, she thought, as she yawned and blinked her sleep-ridden eyes and gazed at the huge expanse of blue water, with the long jetty and yachts and cruisers moored alongside.

Barry opened the door.

'Here we are. First part of your journey over. You tired?'

'Yes. I don't know why, as I slept most of the flight.'

'It affects some folk that way.' He was locking the car, taking out the luggage. 'It does on me. The master, now, he says he wakes up. He reckons he does his best work on the plane. I guess it's 'cos he's not being interrupted. This way, Miss Shaw.'

She followed him, vaguely conscious of the deliberate barrier he had raised between them. Although he was friendly he was also impersonal as if determined to be polite but refusing to chatter or suggest that he was being familiar. She wondered why. Could it be the way all the master's employees behaved? Then she frowned, for now she was getting the habit too, and thinking of Ludovic Fairlie as 'the master'.

They walked down the jetty and went on board the cruiser, which was fairly big and luxuriously comfortable. Jan sat in the stern, near Barry, and watched him, but he was intent on his work and seemed to hardly notice her. She stared round as the cruiser went out of the harbour. She had heard the Reef could be rough, but this time it was beautifully smooth and the water so incredibly blue. There were many boats out, some yachts with lovely gay sails of the most amazing colours, yellow, purple, black, blue, red, even stripes, and it all added to the colourful scene with the background of long stretches of sand and the green lush hills.

'A lot of boats...' she said to Barry, feeling uncomfortable in the silence.

'Yes ... well, this is a famous holiday centre, you know. Most of the islands have hotels or camping sites. Very popular.'

'We're going to an island?' she asked, conscious that it must sound rather odd, admitting that she didn't know just where they were going.

'Barracuda Isle.'

'Why's it called that?'

'Because ... because, I suppose.' He gave an odd smile. 'The master is a fisherman. He caught several huge barracuda here, so I suppose that was why he called the island that. Before he bought it, it was just an island without a name.'

'It's the ... it's Mr Fairlie's island?' Jan asked.

'Of course.'

Barry Ryder turned away as if closing the conversation and Jan looked around her. They were leaving a foam-spray line behind them as they went through the ultramarine-blue water, passing the islands, some covered with trees, a few with small hills. On many of the islands she could see white hotels.

And then they seemed to leave most of the islands behind and moved out into water that was slashed with bursts of white foam as the rollers came in. They were going past one island where trees grew down to the water's edge, their long palm fronds bent, the slender trunks bending away from the wind.

'That's Timton Island,' Barry Ryder told her, 'our nearest neighbour. We have to go right round our island to get to the reef and into the lagoon. Just look ahead and you'll

41

see it. On the far side we have a mountain.'
He grinned. 'Leastways we call it that,
though some disagree and say it's only a hill.
It's unusual to find waterfalls that go into
the sea, but you can here. It's beaut, all
right.'

Jan turned to stare ahead. At first she
could only see the ocean stretching away
into the distance with a heat haze hovering
and then, slowly, almost deliberately, the
island appeared.

Palm trees! She had never seen so many
palm trees before, she thought – tall,
slender, so graceful, and romantic.

The word romantic jerked her to aware-
ness. Why, she had not thought of George
once, all day long! She wondered whether
this meant that she would soon lose the
sense of desolation, the feeling of being
unloved, the loneliness? Would she really
pick up the pieces and start again? And then
she forgot George as she stared and the
island came closer. The waves were racing
up against the coral reef, tossing the surf
high in the air, to fall heavily on the small
crevasses and ravines of the coral. The
cruiser went through the narrow channel
into the calmness of the blue lagoon and she
gazed up at the 'mountain' that dominated

the end of the island.

'Look,' Barry told Jan. 'You don't often see that.'

There was a proud note in his voice as he pointed to the jagged rocks and the crystal clear cascades of water falling down into the receding sea below. As the powerful rollers came racing in, they hid the cascades of water completely until the sea receded again. This was, of course, just outside the coral reef for, once inside it, the water was calm.

'You never been here before?' he asked as he made for the small jetty.

'No. I've only been in Australia six months.'

He looked at her. 'Like it?'

'Love it,' she told him, and it was true. She had loved it – until George. There! Thoughts of George were back again and briefly depression descended on her as she got out of the cruiser and followed Barry Ryder down the short jetty. Vaguely she noticed the earthy road and the mass of trees beyond it. A carriage, with two black horses, was waiting, with an aboriginal sitting above, a wide grin splitting his dark face as he saw them.

Barry shouted something unintelligible and the man jumped down, came to meet them, took the cases and opened the door of the carriage.

Jan wanted to giggle. 'I've never been in one of these before,' she admitted.

Barry glanced at her. 'The master won't allow cars on the island. He prefers to keep it this way.'

'It's rather fun,' Jan confessed, some of her depression lifting as the horses trotted gracefully along the earth road, on one side a mass of trees, on the other the beautiful emerald green lagoon. Then, just before the road made a sharp right turn and she thought they must be on the other side of the island, Barry pointed.

'That's Timton Island … see?'

Jan looked and through the heat haze could just see the island. Then the road they were on straightened and ahead of her she saw a house, a single-storied Colonial-type house with pillars to support the roof of the verandah that ran all the way round. It was built on a mound, overlooking another lagoon.

'There's no channel out of *this* lagoon, so we can't use it,' Barry told her. 'Anyway, it's better this way. Keeps the house quiet, way the master likes it.'

The master, the master, always the master,

Jan thought impatiently. Doesn't anyone else matter? For the first time since she left Sydney, she thought of Jarvis's mother and knew a twinge of anxiety. What sort of woman would Mrs Fairlie be? she wondered. Friendly? Or reserved? Perhaps critical? Or even disapproving?

'It's a beautiful house,' Jan admitted almost reluctantly as the carriage stopped. The front door opened and a dark-skinned woman in a blue frock and starched white apron came outside to collect the luggage and lead the way in. Barry hesitated.

'You'll be glad to have a shower and a rest, Miss Shaw. I'll see you later. Okay?'

'Okay,' Jan agreed, a little puzzled, for after all, she was Mrs Fairlie's guest, not the master's, so why should it be 'okay' to see Barry later?

She followed the maid into a lofty cool hall, bracing herself for the meeting that lay ahead. They walked down a corridor, then the woman opened a door and stood back.

Jan walked through and saw, to her surprise, that she was in a bedroom, a lovely room with one wall all glass, giving a wonderful view of the blue lagoon with the palm trees bending by it, as if to drink the water. A room luxuriously furnished, the bed covered with a pale yellow silk bed-spread which matched the long curtains, a polished floor with a deep green rug by the side of the bed.

Somehow she had expected to be shown into a lounge, or perhaps, in a house like this, it would be called a 'drawing-room', where Mrs Fairlie would be waiting for her.

She glanced round. Her cases had been placed on a small stand, the maid went and opened a door, standing back and beckoning to Jan. It was a small bathroom with a shower.

Jan smiled at her. 'Thanks, I do feel like a shower.'

Perhaps she hadn't understood Barry Ryder, when he surprised her by saying 'a shower and a rest'. Maybe she was expected to take both before meeting Jarvis's mother. That made sense in this hot country, Jan thought. As the maid turned away, Jan realised she had not understood a word she had said.

Once alone, Jan stripped quickly. She *was* hot and sticky. A cool shower certainly helped. When she came out of the bathroom the cover had been taken off the bed, the single sheet turned back. She saw, also, that her suitcase had been unpacked, the clothes hung in the wardrobe.

She pulled on her thin coral-coloured dressing-gown and lay on top of the sheet. The wide verandah shut out the glare of the sunshine and sleep overtook Jan.

When she awoke, some hours later, she was startled at the time. How very rude Mrs Fairlie would think her! Hastily she had another shower which did a lot to remove her drowsiness and dressed carefully, choosing a simple pink frock with a gold chain belt and matching sandals. She brushed her hair carefully, twisting it round her head like a turban. She used make-up very lightly, for she wanted to make a good impression and maybe Jarvis's mother was old-fashioned. If she was anything like her brother-in-law, Jan thought, she would be! At last she was ready. Trying not to feel nervous, she went into the hall.

Everything was quiet, and still. Strangely, almost ominously still, she thought – and then told herself she was being absurd. Perhaps on the island they had the same sort of siesta people had in Spain. Maybe she was too early…

All the doors in the long hall and corridor were closed and she didn't like to open any of them, so she went back into her bedroom and out on to the verandah through the french doors. Here it was still hot but no longer so humid.

The utter beauty of the scene enthralled her and she stood still, staring at the natural grace of the palm trees round the lagoon. She could see the haze hiding Timton Island in the distance and, oddly, no longer felt so alone. She walked along the verandah, giving furtive glances at the rooms she passed.

She could see into each room, and each room was empty. They were beautifully furnished rooms. There was a dining-room with an oval mahogany table and a beautiful sideboard, carved meticulously; and a drawing-room with satinwood furniture and tapestries on the walls. There were also several bedrooms, each as luxurious as her own. But not a single person.

There were chairs round a table on the verandah so she sat down, puzzled, still a little uneasy, for it all had a nightmare quality, unreal, as if...

She heard the soft pad of shoes on the boards of the verandah and the maid stood there. She held out a note.

'Me Lucy,' she said, and turned away.

'Thank you, Lucy,' Jan said, smiling, grateful for even this tiny bit of communication. She opened the note and read it quickly.

'The master has phoned and will join you tomorrow night. He asked me to send you his apologies and hopes you will have a good rest. Unfortunately I can't see you tonight, but will tomorrow.'

It was signed Barry Ryder.

Puzzled, Jan re-read the note. It didn't make sense, she thought, for why a quoted phone message? If Ludovic Fairlie could phone the island, why couldn't he have spoken to her? And what could be the reason Barry Ryder could not see her that night? She wondered; after all, why should he see her, anyway, for she was Mrs Fairlie's guest?

She decided to explore the house. There was no sign of anyone and at one end of the hall was a baize-covered door. It was locked. She knocked on it, but no one answered. She wondered where it led to.

In the drawing-room, she found some books. There were a few modern novels, but none that interested her. However, she couldn't just sit and stare at the lagoon, she decided, so she chose a book and went and sat outside on the verandah again.

The time dragged by and the sun went

down. The house was suddenly ablaze with electric light and Jan went inside. She sat down in the empty drawing-room and waited. Where was Mrs Fairlie? Surely she would soon be there; she couldn't rest for ever.

But Mrs Fairlie did not come. Lucy came instead, ringing a little bell and led the way to the dining-room. Jan ate alone, a tasty well-cooked meal of chicken, and ice-cream which she enjoyed, followed by coffee.

She went back to the drawing-room, bewildered, not sure what to do, for Mrs Fairlie must be *somewhere*.

Lucy was no help. Jan had said slowly, half a dozen times:

'Mrs Fairlie. Mrs Fairlie.'

But the dark face had showed no understanding, so Jan tried something else.

'The master ... the master...'

She was rewarded. Lucy's face split up into a smile, her teeth very white.

'Yes, yes, the master. Good. The master. Good. Tomorrow ... tomorrow,' she said, and left the room.

Jan sighed. That hadn't got her very far, had it? And why, if Lucy understood the words *the master*, had she failed to understand *Mrs Fairlie?*

The night was so quiet – an occasional thud from outside but otherwise still. A fabulous crescent moon, golden in the dark sky, spreading a swathe of golden lava on the calm lagoon. So very lovely...

Somehow it made Jan think of George and she felt the tears returning. Hastily she showered, pulled on her pale pink shortie pyjamas and scrambled into bed. She wept, but not for long. She had expected a restless, unhappy, perhaps fearful night, for she had never felt so alone before, but instead she slept well, only waking when Lucy called her with a tray of fried eggs and bacon, toast and marmalade, and coffee.

'Morning. Eat,' Lucy said, and beamed.

'Thank you.'

Jan realised with surprise that she was hungry.

After showering, she dressed. This time she wore a pale yellow frock and went out on to the verandah. The sun was very bright and the heat oppressive. She sat down and stared at the blue water.

How still everything was, she thought, and the silence went on and on. Even Lucy made no sound as she glided along the floor. Jan felt disturbed, for surely you don't invite someone to stay with you and then not be there? she thought worriedly. There wasn't even a message. At the same time, she could feel some of the tenseness leaving her limbs as she looked about her, for it was so beautiful, so incredibly peaceful.

Remembering the rat race of Sydney, where you fought to get on a bus, or forced your way along George Street through the lunch-hour crowds, it seemed impossible to believe that there could be places like this, she thought. Here everything was not only lovely but so blissfully quiet. A place where you could think.

Now, relaxed and alone, she could look back down the years and remember that she had always been the quiet girl, while Felicity was gay, ambitious and beautiful, the daughter who did things and who didn't sit back and wait, retreating behind Frank, Jan realised. Perhaps that was why she felt so alone now. Frank had been like her, in so many ways – shy, finding it hard to mix; perhaps he had been as grateful for her friendship as she had been for his. Life had gone smoothly, seemed so perfect until one day she woke up and saw him as he really was: a childhood friend. She had told him nervously, afraid of hurting him, and had been even more hurt when he agreed and she knew he didn't love her, either. He had provided the security she needed.

Jan leaned back on the chair, her feet up, a delicious drowsiness seeping through her, as she went on thinking about the past; perhaps being frank with herself for the first time. Was it surprising, she asked herself, if on coming out to Australia, where Felicity had Jarvis and soon made friends, Jan had found herself caught up in a new loneliness? A loneliness of being unloved. No mum to rush home to – no Frank next door to go to if she wanted to see a certain film or felt like dancing. She was completely alone, she had felt. Small wonder that George had seemed like the answer to her prayer.

It had all been her fault, she thought, and not George's, for she had been in the right mood for him. Flattered by his attention, thrilled because for once the girls in the office envied her, it had all gone to her head. Perhaps that was why she had built it up into a bigger emotional relationship than George had had in mind. Maybe that was why his tactful handling of the situation had hurt her far more than it would have done, normally. Well, all that was in the past and the sooner she forgot George, with his intriguing smile, that smooth charm, the better. She jumped up. The perspiration broke out all over her. Showering, she told herself, was the only answer, so she went to her room.

Later she went to sit down again, wondering when Mrs Fairlie would appear. Was this – could this be a deliberate act? Was Jarvis's mother being rude on purpose, to make it plain that Jan was an unwelcome guest? But if so, why had Mrs Fairlie invited her in the first place? And then she thought of something else; could it have been Ludovic Fairlie's idea? Was it all a lie, Mrs Fairlie's invitation? Yet how could it be, for there had been the letter from Mrs Fairlie herself.

Jan suddenly felt the silence was too much for her, so she went out into the sunshine, feeling the heat burning her face and arms. The garden was beautiful. Never before had she seen such colours as the wild purple of the climbing plants, the pale pink of the hibiscus flowers, the deep red of poinsettias with their quaintly pointed branches, looking more like dancers than bushes. Despite the heat, she wandered down on to the soft sand, near the water. There were fascinating tiny pools in which brightly coloured, strange shaped little fish swam.

Here there was so much colour that it was

vivid, eye-catching, and yet somehow har-
monised by the pale blue cloudless sky and
the incredible loveliness of the sea. Maybe
that was why she was feeling happier, she
thought, as she strolled back to the house,
realising it would be foolish to stay in the
sunshine too long. Perhaps the beauty
around her was enveloping her, even comforting her, reassuring her about the future.
She no longer felt afraid, nor did the silence
of the empty house alarm her. Instead she
welcomed it. Everything was so still and
quiet with no one to hurt her, just herself.

As she sat on the verandah, she suddenly
understood everything. Ludovic Fairlie
would be there that evening, bringing his
sister-in-law with him. That would explain
his apologies and her absence. Perhaps they
had planned this visit so that Mrs Fairlie
and her beloved Jarvis's 'girl-friend' could
be alone in this intimate stillness and so
grow to know one another far better than
they could ever have done in the noise and
crowds of Sydney. Soon Ludovic Fairlie and
his sister-in-law would be with her and this
beautiful peace would have gone, so why
not enjoy it now? she asked herself.

Lucy arrived with a jug of iced lemon and
a glass.

'Eat. Soon,' said Lucy, looking proud of her English.

Jan smiled back, wondering how hard Lucy's own language would be to learn.

She ate the salmon and salad with enjoyment and was startled when Barry Ryder joined her afterwards. He seemed stiff and unfriendly, but very polite – too polite, so Jan wondered if she had unconsciously offended him. She had already learned how sensitive Australians were and how often they failed to understand English humour.

She told him of her walk in the garden.

'You keep it beautifully.'

'It's my job.'

'The whole island is so lovely,' she went on, refusing to be snubbed. 'I'm longing to explore it.'

'It's for the master to show you,' Barry said coldly.

Jan stared at him. Had he a wife? she wondered. Everything in the house was so still, so silent. It was almost as if no one dared make a sound. Was that the effect the master had on them? Even when he wasn't there? she thought.

And why, if Barry had a wife, who lived in the house, surely she could have welcomed Jan, even talked to her a little, asking if everything was all right? Jan thought.

Barry himself seemed to act strangely at times, so perhaps his wife was the same. He could be friendly and then quite suddenly his voice became formal, almost stiff. There was something funny somewhere.

And then Barry spoke, almost as if he could read her thoughts.

'My wife and I have our own self-contained flat in the house, but keep to ourselves. The master likes it that way,' he said. 'And so do we,' he added, but in such a way that Jan wondered if he was telling the whole truth.

'The master sounds an impossible man,' Jan said. 'Why is it always what *he* likes?'

'He pays the bills.' Barry stood up, giving her an odd little smile and turning to go.

'Barry, please...' Jan put her hand to stop him 'where is Mrs Fairlie?'

He looked surprised at the question.

'Out on one of her trips, of course. That's where she is mostly, you know.'

Then he hurried away.

But she didn't know, Jan thought, as she watched him go. *Out on one of her trips,* Barry had said of Mrs Fairlie. Trips? What trips? Jan wondered. Still, that added up to what she had thought and accepted. When

Ludovic Fairlie arrived, he would bring his sister-in-law with him.

Jan was sitting on the verandah when Ludovic Fairlie arrived. She was totally unprepared, for somehow she had expected to see the carriage, so she sat still, just staring at the white horse that came trotting along the earth road, with Ludovic on his back.

Jan's first thought was *where* was Mrs Fairlie? And then Ludovic was off his horse as a small boy came running to take the horse away, and Ludovic was walking towards her – just as she remembered him, tall, broadshouldered, with that rather amused, condescending smile.

'Settled in all right?' he asked, standing by her side. 'What do you think of it?'

His voice was friendly and she reacted unconsciously.

'I think it's fabulous. I've never seen any place so beautiful,' she told him warmly.

'I'm glad you like it.' He smiled at her. 'Mind if I shower and change into something cooler?'

'Of course not,' she said. He must be hot, she thought, in that neat dark suit.

When he had gone, she sat very still, her hands folded neatly in her lap, but her brain seemed in a turmoil. She just couldn't understand it. Where was Mrs Fairlie? After all, Jan thought, Mrs Fairlie was supposed to be her hostess.

Supposed to be...? The words stayed in her mind. Yet it didn't make sense. Why should Ludovic Fairlie want to get her here? Why...

Life seemed to be full of that question: 'Why?' she thought, when Ludovic returned, cool, his hair still wet from the shower, his suit replaced by thin khaki shorts and open-necked shirt. Lucy came hurrying with a tray and cold drinks, and Ludovic relaxed in a low wicker chair with a sigh of relief.

'I always feel happy here,' he said.

Jan stared at him. How content he looked, how different from the stern unfriendly man who had called at her flat.

'You don't find it too quiet?' she asked him.

He turned his head.

'Certainly not. Here I can think. Do you find it quiet? Too quiet?'

'I did at first,' she confessed. 'It was sort of eerie. No one to talk to ... no one at all...' She looked at him. 'I haven't met Mrs Fairlie yet.'

He looked amused.

'Haven't you? Oh dear, my sister-in-law is so unstable. She's probably on one of her tours and has forgotten about you. But she'll be back soon. You'll meet her, don't worry.'

Jan felt a sudden stirring inside of annoyance.

'I should hope so, seeing she invited me here!' she began.

Ludovic was packing his pipe. What long fingers he had, she thought, what strong hands. Somehow he looked like an outdoor man, not an executive of a big stockbrokers. Executive and probably chief stockholder, she thought, for he must be very wealthy to be able to fly up here for a quiet weekend and have such a lovely place. It must cost a fortune to run this island ... and those cars, and he was sure to have his own plane.

Now he looked at her, his eyes narrowed.

'I think it's best that we be frank, Jan.'

She was startled, for his voice had changed. It had lost the warm friendliness and become the harsh voice he had used when he called at her flat.

'Frank?' she echoed.

He nodded.

'Yes, frank. I want you to know that while we have nothing against you as a person, both Jarvis's mother and I strongly disapprove of this romance. Of any romance where Jarvis is concerned, I must add.'

Jan twisted her fingers together tightly.

'Surely Jarvis is old enough...'

'That's the point. He's not! He may be twenty years old, but he's immature and definitely not ready for marriage.'

He paused and she just stopped herself from nodding, for she was in complete agreement. Jarvis was young, far too young for the responsibilities of being a husband, and perhaps later, a father. But she could not admit this or Ludovic might get suspicious, and as long as she could let him believe that she was Jarvis's 'love' it gave Jarvis freedom to be in love with Felicity.

'Jarvis is like his father – my brother. Weak, easily fooled, enjoys life and expects everything to be handed to him on a silver platter...' Ludovic went on, his voice stern. 'Jarvis never bothered to work at school. I doubt if he works at the university.' He put up his hand as Jan began to speak. 'Let me finish. His mother is anxious about him. Jarvis's father broke her heart with his irresponsible behaviour. Our firm nearly went bankrupt because of his lack of knowledge and complete indifference. Jarvis will

61

eventually inherit the business, but he has to be trained so that he can run it correctly. That's why it's vitally important that he pass his exams.'

'Does he want to inherit the firm?' she asked, unable to keep silent.

Ludovic's mouth twisted bitterly.

'I have no idea. *I* didn't want to join the firm, but when Jarvis's father made such a mess of it, my father was sick and he sent for me. I'm a grazier, I loathe office life and the rat race, but it was my duty. When Jarvis is twenty-five he can sell it if he wishes to do so, but there's his mother to consider. Most of her income derives from the firm. She is Jarvis's responsibility – mine at the moment, of course. But Jarvis must grow up, cease to be a playboy, expecting everything to come to him without any effort on his part.'

'And you think marriage – or an engagement – would stop Jarvis from working?' Jan was amused. 'Aren't you being rather Victorian? Lots of men marry young and become famous and successful.'

Ludovic did not smile.

'Maybe, but they're not Jarvis. He is obviously very infatuated with you, and unless you're out of the way, Jarvis will fail his exams.'

'Out of the way?' Jan repeated the words. Ludovic was smiling.

'Don't look so terrified. I'm not using the expression in the way Westerns do. Honestly, you amaze me. I'm not going to murder you, merely keep you here, out of Jarvis's way. But you're free to go, any time.'

She tried to smile, but there was an emptiness inside her as she stared at him.

'I thought you were going to keep me here as a prisoner?'

Ludovic laughed. He poured her a fresh cold drink.

'You love being dramatic, don't you? A willing prisoner, shall we say. If you love Jarvis, you'll want to help him and not destroy him. If you stay here and Jarvis is free to work, content because he knows you're here, that he need not be jealous, wonder with whom you are, you'll be proving your love for him, and this might considerably affect my opinion of you – and that of his mother.'

He paused, staring at the pale face of the girl, who was looking at him as if she was stunned.

'Well?' he asked. 'Do you love Jarvis enough to stay here and give him a chance?'

She shook her head; her mind seemed muddled.

'Look, first let's get something straight. I've never kept Jarvis from studying. We didn't go out all that much together.'

Ludovic was smiling, but without amusement this time.

'Jarvis told his mother a very different tale. He said he was worried about his work because he couldn't concentrate. That he had to see you, because he was jealous. That he knew he was too possessive, but...'

'Jarvis said that?' Jan was startled. She could not believe it. It wasn't like Jarvis. Why, even when Felicity had been around Jarvis had never been possessive or jealous, nor had he haunted Felicity all the time. Felicity had even once complained because he didn't see her enough!

'Yes. He also said that he was eager to pass his exams well but that when you were so wholeheartedly in love, it was difficult to concentrate,' Ludovic went on.

Jan drew a long deep breath. Either Ludovic was inventing all this – and if he was, why? Or Jarvis... Suddenly she understood. Jarvis was scared lest he fail his exams and was preparing his mother in advance, blaming it on to a love affair that was, in fact, non-existent.

'I have proof also that you and Jarvis

spend a lot of time together,' Ludovic went on slowly.

'You mean...' Jan's temper rose swiftly. 'You mean you actually spied on us?'

Ludovic was smiling.

'How dramatic! I didn't "spy", I merely had you followed.'

'Why split hairs?' She jumped up, so angry she couldn't speak for a moment. 'You had no right!'

He stood up, his hands tight and hard on her arms.

'I have every right. I'm Jarvis's guardian. I want to help him. My sister-in-law and I have discussed the matter carefully and we both came to the conclusion that you're the only person who can help Jarvis – by being kept out of his way.'

She moved swiftly, dislodging his hands.

'By being kept out of his way?' she echoed angrily. 'In other words, I *am* a prisoner. You kidnapped me. You never told me this. If I'd known...'

'You wouldn't have come?'

He seemed so huge as he looked down at her, but her anger gave her courage.

'If you'd made me understand, I might have come of my own free will, but...'

'You're here of your own free will,' he told

her, and sat down. 'Do stop being melodramatic. Sit down and pour me another drink. If you want to, you can go home tomorrow.'

There was what seemed to Jan an endless silence. She stood still, just staring at him. And he stared back, a little smile playing round his mouth.

'You mean that?'

Her voice was squeaky, she noticed with dismay, but the anger was seeping out of her.

'Of course I mean it. You can go home tomorrow. I hope you won't, though. If you do, I shall have to take more drastic measures.'

Jan sank into the chair, her hands clutching the wicker arms.

'So you're still threatening me?'

He smiled. 'Not you, merely the man you're suppose to love.'

'What could you do to Jarvis?'

She leaned forward, hating him, hating his smug face, his amused voice, his eyes that could be so cold and the next moment surprisingly warm.

'Lots of things. I could halve his allowance. That he'd hate. His car is actually mine. I might need it.'

'This is moral blackmail. Jarvis is a man, not a child. You've no right...'

'As I said before, I have every right. I'm his guardian.'

Jan took a deep breath.

'Jarvis could get a job – a job he likes, work he enjoys.'

She was startled by Ludovic's roar of laughter. She sat still, just staring at him as he laughed and laughed. When he stopped, she waited until he spoke.

'Jan, how old are you? Or are you wilfully deceiving yourself? Can you see Jarvis in a job? Can you imagine him clocking in each morning? You know what a clock-watcher he'd be. He's weak as jelly.' Ludovic's voice was scornful. 'Somehow we've got to teach him not to be. No sane man would employ a long-haired irresponsible kid like Jarvis. We've got to teach him what work is. His mother needs a man to look after her, and Jarvis is a long way from being a man.'

Jan looked down at her hands. Actually she agreed with every word Ludovic had said. Jarvis was not a man. Jarvis would never be able to accept the discipline of a job. All the same...

'Couldn't you have done it a different way?' she asked.

Ludovic finished his drink.

'How?'

'Well, by telling me all this in Sydney? Discussing it with Jarvis. You did see him.'

Ludovic smiled.

'Yes. I took him out to dinner as I guessed you'd phone him.' He looked amused. 'Be your age, Jan. Can you imagine Jarvis agreeing docilely to losing his darling little Jan? Can you see yourself agreeing to tear yourself away from such a prize?'

'Prize?'

Ludovic chuckled.

'Oh, please, Jan, you can't be as naïve as all that. You must know that Jarvis is one of the most eligible bachelors in Sydney.'

Her cheeks burning, Jan was on her feet again.

'Are you suggesting...'

And he was on his feet, his hands on her arms again, as he shook her.

'Do stop being dramatic. All I'm asking you to do is to stay here for a few months and give my nephew a chance to study for his exams. Is that so much? A free holiday in this beauty spot... Is that hard to accept? If you really love Jarvis.'

Jan's hands went up to her head, for her hair was toppling down. It was difficult to be dignified when she knew she must look so funny.

'All right,' she said suddenly. 'I'll stay, but if Jarvis fails his exams, don't blame me. It's because he hates the work. It has nothing to do with me.'

Ludovic stood back, letting his hands fall to his sides.

'I think you're being a little too modest, Jan. Jarvis is an impressionable young man. You're a very attractive girl. I'm not surprised that he fell in love with you.'

Jan caught her breath. Staring up at Ludovic, she could hardly believe her ears. A compliment like that! she thought.

But then Ludovic turned away, adding:

'Of course you're not every man's type.'

At that moment Lucy appeared. She spoke to Ludovic in a language that could have been anything.

'Dinner, Jan. Hungry?'

Ludovic's voice was impersonal, polite as to a visitor, disinterested but formal.

'Yes ... a little.'

Jan felt embarrassed and confused. For a moment she had thought Ludovic found her attractive. The knowledge that she wasn't his type had hurt rather than surprised her. But then Ludovic wasn't *her* type, either, she thought as she followed him to the dining-room, so that made them equal.

He talked, through an exquisite dinner which both obviously enjoyed, of the island.

'I'll show you around tomorrow. I don't want you to get bored here, Jan, and there's so much to see.'

It was after they had coffee in the drawing-room that Ludovic excused himself.

'I have to bring a certain amount of work with me, otherwise I couldn't get my week-ends off. I find I get through a great deal more here than in Sydney. By the way...' He paused at the doorway and looked at her. She saw the amusement in his eyes and she tensed, preparing herself for whatever he had to say. 'By the way, Jan, don't be concerned for your reputation. You're not alone in the house with me. Barry and his wife have a flat here.'

'I know. Barry told me.'

'Indeed? You haven't met his wife?'

'No. I ... well, I rather wondered why.'

'They like to keep to themselves, and I agree. It's the most harmonious way of living. She runs the house very well indeed and Barry is my right hand.'

'But doesn't she get lonely here?'

Ludovic looked surprised.

'Lonely? I've never thought of it.' He opened the door and looked at her. 'I've never been lonely in my life,' he said as he closed the door.

CHAPTER TWO

The island was a new, strange and very lovely world, Jan found, as Ludovic, in one of his good moods, friendly, approachable, and not inclined to laugh at her, showed her round. He told her to wear shorts and a shirt, and sneakers.

'The coral can damage your feet badly,' he explained.

When she joined him in the lofty cool hall, he gave her a pointed yellow straw hat.

'Better keep that on. Sunshine is deceptive, especially to a Pommie,' he said with a grin, but it was a friendly smile, not a mocking one.

First they wandered round the beautiful garden and Ludovic showed her the poinsettia, hibiscus, and all the lovely tropical flowers. There was a heady perfume in the air and everything was so colourful that Jan laughed.

'You must be tired of hearing me say "How absolutely gorgeous"!'

The tall man strolling by her side glanced

down at her.

'Not at all. After all, it is my garden.'

He smiled as he spoke but, for a moment, she remembered that it was all his and that he was 'the master'. Why did she resent the thought? she wondered. After all, it wasn't his fault he was so rich, so why should she mind?

It was only another example of the conflicting emotions he aroused in her. At one moment she liked him very much, at another she found herself almost hating him. He could be so friendly and pleasant, and then suddenly arrogant and sarcastic. It was rather like walking a tightrope and she found herself tense as she waited for his change of moods.

But on that perfect day with the graceful palm trees leaning away from the wind, their fronds moving gently, the blue cloudless sky and the incredibly beautiful sea, she found Ludovic at his best.

He showed her the way through the woods, a mass of trees with narrow flat paths between them and cream, fragrant flowers climbing over the branches. The birds fluttered softly, all making different sounds, for some cooing, some trilling. She even heard a strange harsh note and glanced up through the green leaves to the distant sky. But what colours! The birds were like small parakeets, emerald green, blue with streaks of gold.

'This is a short cut through to the lagoon,' Ludovic explained. 'You won't want to send for the carriage every time you go fossicking.'

'Fossicking?' she echoed. She had been looking at two lovely large red and yellow butterflies lying flatly on white flowers that looked like magnolias.

He grinned, his hand under her elbow for a moment as he helped her step over a fallen trunk of a tree.

'That's what we call searching the reef. I'm going to introduce you to Rab Mortimer. He's a naturalist and comes over here every day. I've given permission.'

The words riled Jan for a moment. 'I've given permission' sounded so arrogant and pompous, and then she scolded herself silently. After all, the island *was* Ludovic's and he had every right to refuse to let every Tom, Dick and Harry come here whenever they liked. If he didn't, the island would be overrun by unwanted tourists, for surely it must be the most beautiful island of them all.

'Yes, he collects specimens for his lab. I think you'll like him and find it interesting. Fascinating, in fact. You'll need gloves, though, for you meet some horrible creatures that can sting severely. Ever done any underwater swimming?'

They were walking through the trees slowly, the sweet scent with them, the birds chattering all round. Jan looked up eagerly.

'No, but I've always longed to.'

'Good. On my next visit, I'll bring up the gear and teach you. You'll find it fun.'

'I'd love that...' Jan began eagerly, and then paused. 'On my next visit', he'd said. Somehow it had a strangely ominous sound, for how long would he be away? How long was she expected to stay there? she wondered, and then scolded herself again for worrying. Until Jarvis had taken his exams, of course. After all, she could go when she liked, for she was not a prisoner, so why should she mind staying here in this lovely spot? Wasn't it a million times nicer than that little Kings Cross flat in Sydney where she had sat, lonely, weeping for her lost love? George!

She caught her breath. It was nearly twenty-four hours since she had thought of him, she realised, so did that mean she was forgetting him? She hoped so – and surely this was the best place to do it?

She stopped abruptly, seeing some strange objects dangling from the branches of the trees.

'What are they?'

'Flying foxes ... or fruit bats as some call them. Never seen one before?'

'Never.' Jan went to stand below them, looking up at the bodies hanging, head down and very motionless. 'What weird looking-creatures. Do they sleep all day like bats?' She peered up at them. She could not see much but that their faces looked just like those of small foxes. She turned to Ludovic impulsively. 'This is the most exciting place I've ever been to!'

He laughed. 'You haven't seen anything yet!'

Later, as they sat on the warm sand under the palm trees, watching the water as it broke over the reef in huge white waves, they talked – of Sydney, of Lewes where she lived. Jan found herself telling him about her mother, who was a widow.

'She's absolutely wonderful. Dad died when we were quite young, but Mum brought us up. Now she has this boutique and is doing very well.'

'She must miss you.'

'She never says so,' Jan gave a little shrug. 'We went to boarding school and she got used to being alone. She's always been very keen on us being independent.'

'You have a brother?'

'No, a sister.'

Even as she said the word, Jan regretted it. So long as Ludovic knew nothing about Felicity, he would not worry about Jarvis, believing him safe with Jan out of the way! But it was too late, for he was looking at her.

'A sister?'

'Yes,' Jan kept her voice casual. 'Felicity. She's up north at the moment.'

'I see.'

'Oh, look!' Jan said quickly, scrambling to her feet, pointing. She had been looking for some way to change the conversation and, miraculously, these had appeared.

Several long sleek black dolphins were leaping out of the water, twisting their bodies, looking as if they were having a wonderful time.

'Aren't they graceful?' Jan exclaimed as she hurried down towards the water's edge.

Together they walked along the sand towards the coral reef. She had heard so much about the coral that protected lagoons and was supposed to be so lovely that for a moment she was disappointed as the reef looked a drab waste-land, but then, as they came closer, she caught her breath with delight as she saw the fairyland of colour. There were patches of vividly purple coral, also grey pointed fingers, topped with palest pink which were side by side with pale pink fingers, and again there were green fingers so that it was a varied splash of beauty.

'It looks so different when you're not near it,' Jan said.

Ludovic glanced down at her with a smile.

'Doesn't that apply to most things? It doesn't do to judge anything or anyone until you get a close look at them?' His voice was friendly, but there was a significant note in it that made her turn to stare at him. He was smiling at her. 'Take you, for example,' he went on. 'You're totally different from what I imagined you would be. I needed this close view to see the real you.'

'I am?' She was startled. 'Just what did you expect?'

'Well, in the first place, I thought of Jarvis's other girl-friends – all glamour girls but painfully dumb. You're quite different.'

'Painfully unglamorous and talkative?' she said with an impish smile.

'Certainly not. You're both glamorous and intelligent. I just can't understand what you see in Jarvis.'

Jan turned round abruptly.

'Why do you always knock poor Jarvis?' she asked, her temper rising. 'He's young and immature, but so were you – once.'

'I sincerely hope not!' Ludovic said firmly, his eyes amused. 'Do you really think I was ever like Jarvis?'

Jan looked at him thoughtfully, at his crisply-white shorts, the immaculate shirt, the short bleached hair, the face with his squarish chin, shrewd eyes, firm mouth. She had to be honest as the warm sun caressed her back and the soft call of the birds made a pleasantly relaxing melody which mingled with the roar of the waves.

'No, I don't,' she admitted. 'But you must have gone through that difficult age.'

'Yes, I was difficult,' he agreed, to her surprise. 'But in a different way. I wanted to farm. Father was against it, so I rebelled. I only came back, as I told you, because my elder brother let my father down and I was needed. Jarvis, now...'

'Yes, Jarvis.' Jan faced him, her legs slightly apart, her hands on her hips. 'Just exactly what have you against Jarvis?'

79

'Well, in the first place, he expects life to be easy. He resents discipline, self-administered or otherwise. He wants a good time but isn't prepared to work for it.'

'But that's no different from the average boy of his age,' Jan said earnestly. 'Can't you see that? I know Jarvis is weak, but he's at a difficult age and he lacks self-confidence. Perhaps he's scared of you and afraid he'll let you down.'

Ludovic laughed. 'Scared of me? Who'd be scared of me?'

Jan didn't smile. 'I could be.'

Ludovic's laughter vanished. 'What do you mean? You could be?'

She clasped her hands together and looked down at them. Should she be frank or would he be angry. Then she looked up and saw he was not angry, nor sarcastic, just waiting for her reply.

'Because I never know where I am with you. One moment you're friendly and in a good mood, the next you're being sarcastic and … and domineering.'

Ludovic looked so surprised that Jan wanted to laugh, but didn't.

'Is that how I appear to you? Moody?'

'No, not moody,' she corrected him carefully, 'but a man of many moods. That's

80

quite different.'

'Well...' For a moment he sounded disgruntled and then he smiled. 'Maybe that's my charm. If I've got any, that is.'

'Oh, you have,' Jan said earnestly. She spoke with the naïve honesty of youth and did not notice Ludovic's quick suspicious glance that changed to a rather amused look, for he saw she meant it. 'You've plenty of charm – when you want to use it. I should think you've masses of girl-friends.'

He laughed at that.

'Not masses, but enough. Sometimes too many. Being wealthy has its drawbacks, you know, Jan.'

'I can't imagine any. Just think how wonderful it would be to be rich...' she said, her eyes dreamy. 'Think of all the things you could do with it. Helping people, building houses for old folk, adopting babies and paying for their education. I think it would be simply smashing.'

'You do? You don't want a mink coat or diamonds?'

She knew he was teasing her, but she answered the question seriously.

'I don't suppose I'd refuse them, but I wouldn't be happy. I'd always be scared stiff lest I lost them,' she told him.

He glanced at his watch and whistled softly.

'How time flies! We'd better get back, we're late for lunch. Not that it matters. It's sure to be cold.'

They walked along through the narrow lanes between the trees.

'Rab Mortimer is coming over this afternoon to meet you,' Ludovic said as the long white house came into view. 'I think you'll find him interesting.'

Rab Mortimer, the naturalist, proved to be a rather insignificant-looking man with sandy-coloured hair, a pale freckled face and a shy smile. A short man, Jan thought, as Ludovic introduced them, but a friendly one.

'I'm from England, too, Miss Shaw,' Rab said after a quick glance at Ludovic. 'You're interested in fossicking?'

Jan laughed. She and Ludovic had walked up from the lagoon, eaten a delicious lunch of cold chicken and salad under the gently waving palm trees, then she had had a brief siesta before joining the two men. She was wearing her white frock with the gold chain belt and sandals to match, but she doubted if either man noticed her clothes or even her. They were polite, even charming, but they had been engrossed in their talk about coral and clams.

'I'd never heard the word before Ludovic said it,' Jan confessed. 'I haven't a clue, but it sounds fabulous.'

'Rab'll initiate you into its mysteries,' Ludovic told her. 'He comes over every day.'

'Believe me, I'm grateful, Fairlie. I know how you feel about trespassers.'

Ludovic smiled.

'You didn't trespass. You wrote and asked my permission, Rab. That's the difference. You can imagine how overrun with ghastly tourists we'd be if I didn't make a veto.'

Rab laughed. 'I most certainly can! The tourists are like ants, swarming everywhere with their ghastly transistors, bottles of beer and shrieks of laughter.'

Ludovic nodded.

'Exactly. I want to keep this island the peaceful place it is.'

Later, much later, when Rab had left them, Ludovic asked Jan what she thought of Rab.

'He seems quite nice,' she said truthfully, looking up at the man who towered above her and above Rab.

She thought suddenly that when Ludovic

was in a room, the walls seemed to come creeping closer for he was so big. Not fat, most certainly not, for he had the leanness of a healthy active man. But it wasn't only the physical side of Ludovic that seemed to dominate everything – perhaps it was his aliveness, the vitality, or the certainty in his mind that he was always right, always the strong one, always the master! He seemed to fill the room, make everyone else diminish in size. Certainly Rab Mortimer was like a shadow in comparison.

They spent a pleasant evening, just Ludovic and Jan, talking. He did most of the talking, but she was more than content to listen, for his colourful description of his life as a grazier fascinated her.

'Everything out here is so different, so much bigger,' she said, and paused. Even the men, or Ludovic, were bigger in every way. She thought of Frank, the man she had loved from her childhood – why, he was just a quiet ordinary man in comparison. Even George whom she had loved in Sydney could never hope to equal Ludovic, for all his smooth sophisticated charm. Ludovic seemed to stand alone, to be unique.

She said goodnight to him reluctantly, for she had enjoyed every moment of the day.

She wished Ludovic was always like this; friendly, kind and willing to communicate with her. The side she hated and that roused her to quick often unreasonable anger was his arrogant dominant manner, his changes of mood, his sarcastic amusement at her expense. If only he was always like this!

When she awoke next day with the arrival of her breakfast, she knew that he had already left the island and gone back to the mainland to fly down to Sydney. He did it so casually – to him a thousand miles or even more was the equivalent of a journey of ten miles in England. Out here distances seemed to mean nothing at all, perhaps because they had learned to live with and to accept these incredible distances between cities.

The sun welcomed her as she went outside after a shower. She had dressed for this new game of fossicking in blue Bermuda shorts, white shirt, the yellow pointed straw hat on top of her dark hair that she had tied back in a ponytail. Sneakers were on her bare feet, and the thick gloves Ludovic had given her to wear on her hands.

She walked slowly through the woods, looking up at the sleeping flying foxes, at the huge white flowers, the fragrant yellow flowers of the climbers, listening to the soft enchanting beauty of it all.

Never had she imagined there could be so much beauty. She wished her mother could see it. How she would love the sunshine, the vivid colours, the quietness. And Felicity? Would she love it? Jan wondered, and decided that while her sister might appreciate the beauty of it all, the silence and quietness would seem to her too static to bear. Felicity had to have people round her, laughter, voices, admiring eyes – she had never liked quietness and hated to be alone.

Today Jan was not going to be alone, she thought happily, as she came out from under the shade of the trees and saw the earth road and then the lagoon beyond it. The lagoon was oval, the water an exquisite emerald green today, the wide expanses of coral on either side looked drab from where she was, but she went forward eagerly, remembering her delight the day before when she came across the exquisite pastel colours as well as vivid shades which you only saw close to it.

Rab was there. But was it Rab? Jan wondered, as she crossed the hot sand towards him. He looked so different! Today he wore crumpled shorts and no shirt, his chest going red in the hot sunshine, his straw hat pushed back. She saw his hair was red, not the sandy shade she had thought. He turned to greet her, she saw that his eyes were green and bright with interest. He wore gloves. He had a deep narrow basket on the coral reef by his side, a stick in his hand. Slung over one shoulder was a camera. She also saw a long-handled diamond-shaped net.

'Hi,' he welcomed her. 'Oversleep?'

Even his voice sounded different, much more alive and eager.

That was when she realised something. She had noticed when Barry had come to see Ludovic the day before, as well. Ludovic overshadowed every other man, made them look like shadows, even diminishing their characters.

Rab on his own looked tall. If she was five foot seven inches and he was so high above her now he must be six foot, at least.

Jan wondered if the men knew the effect Ludovic had on their appearance, and if they resented it. Though, perhaps, that was foolish, since it wasn't Ludovic's fault – it was simply because he was made that way. Different.

That day Rab introduced her into an exciting new world and, despite the heat, Jan enjoyed her new life. He showed her how to choose specimens, how to recognise the different species. He even let her photograph some of the coral polyps. He made her feel part of his work, talking as they went, explaining why he wanted different specimens.

'Watch your step carefully, Jan,' he said. 'Coral is brittle and abrasive and can injure you quite seriously, especially if you fall and graze your leg or hands. Never hurry.'

Close behind him, she waded knee-deep in the warm water. As he showed her the beauty of the coral her eyes seemed to grow wider and wider with amazement.

'Such wonderful colours,' she said. 'I wish Mum could see them. She runs a boutique and is crazy about colour.'

She stared at an enormous purple-fringed coral that looked like the head of a cauliflower.

Rab took her to the outer edge of the reef.

'It's easier walking here,' he said, giving her a hand over the difficult parts.

Out here the huge waves came racing in, to burst into a cascade of diamond-flashing drops of water as they hit the reef. It was high tide and the small waterfalls from the tiny mountain had vanished.

'When the tide is out, there are crystal-clear pools of water here,' Rab told her, bending to examine a coral polyp carefully, 'and you see the most beautiful little fishes.'

'What sort?'

'Damselfish.'

She laughed, thinking he was joking, but he grinned.

'True. They have some odd names for things here. Damselfish, butterflies, surgeons, wrasses...'

'Are there sharks?'

Jan was looking out at the ocean with the rollers racing in and shivered.

'They don't often come into the lagoon, but you'd be crazy to swim in the sea.' Rab led the way, talking over his shoulder. 'You do get salt water crocs, though. Not here, usually in estuaries or mangrove swamps. Fairlie's a great one for shooting crocs. He's got quite a name for it.'

'Has he?'

The poor croc, Jan caught herself thinking, and then smiled ruefully. Surely it was better to shoot crocodiles than let them eat people? she thought. Why must she always jump to the conclusion that whatever Ludovic did was wrong? Wrong, at least, in *her* eyes.

Back on the sands, they relaxed for a while, Jan scolding Rab for not wearing a shirt.

'You know how susceptible redheads are to the sun.'

He turned to look at her.

'I'm trying to get tanned like Fairlie.'

'Like Ludovic? You haven't a chance,' Jan laughed. 'What hope have you? He's been tanned every summer of his life. We, coming out from England, have to start from scratch.'

'Tell me,' Rab said, 'what do you make of Ludovic Fairlie? To me, as a dumb quiet-living Pommie, he's unique, a ... well,' he laughed, 'I like to work out what makes people tick, but I can't find what makes him. Do you know him well?'

'Hardly at all. I know his nephew, Jarvis, better.'

'Jarvis Fairlie? Yes, I've heard of him. Nothing like his uncle, is he? Bit of a play-boy.'

'He's young...' Jan began indignantly, and stopped as she saw Rab smile.

'Waving the flag for him?'

Her cheeks were hot for a moment.

'No, it's just that it maddens me the way all you older men run down young ones.

Jarvis is only twenty – you can't expect him to settle down without...'

'Sowing his wild oats? I gather he's sown more than his fair share,' Rab laughed again. 'Look, I'm only twenty-nine. Do you put me in a class with the oldies?'

She blushed again. 'I didn't mean to... I was thinking of Ludovic...'

'I reckon he's only about thirty, maybe thirty-two. How old are you?'

'Nineteen.'

Rab laughed.

'You look more like thirteen,' he said, and added hastily: 'At least today. Yesterday you looked older. Amazing the difference clothes and smart hairdo's make. Today you look like a kid.'

She laughed. 'You look about seventeen in that get-up, Rab.'

Somehow she didn't mind him teasing and laughing at her. It was different when Ludovic...

She jumped up. 'Come and have lunch with me...' she began, then stopped. In a way, she was in an awkward position. Had she the right, as a guest, to invite someone else to lunch? she wondered.

Rab saved the situation by refusing.

'I always bring sandwiches and after lunch

go back to the mainland. I've a lot of work to do in the lab.' He stood up and held out his hand. 'It's been great fun having you around, Jan. Sometimes the silence here gets oppressive. See you tomorrow morning?'

'Of course,' she said, and smiled.

As she began to go into the shadow of the tall trees she glanced round. Rab was bent over his notebook, writing furiously. He had already forgotten her.

The lunch was waiting, delicious as usual. Lucy smiled as she served it and experimented with words, Jan trying to repeat what Lucy said, Lucy doing the same. Then Lucy vanished and the rest of the day stretched ahead. The quietness of the house was strange, almost eerie, Jan thought again as she wandered from room to room. It was all so beautiful – and yet so... Looking round her, she searched for the right word. Unlived-in? Was that the word? Cold? Unnatural? It was so beautiful it might be a picture from one of the glossy magazines – the sort of pictures that drew admiration but made most people shudder at the thought of having to live in such a place.

Ludovic had shown her the record player and a library of records, and how to work the radio, also some books in case she wanted to read.

She drifted through the silent, hushed rooms to her bedroom, showered, and lay down on her bed, her hands under her head.

How rarely she thought of George these days, she realised. In a way, this visit to the Isle was a great help. It was making her forget George and her heartache. Now she could look back on the brief love affair with clearer vision. She could think of George with his sophisticated charm, his insistence on taking her to the most expensive restaurants, the best seats at the theatre, almost as if he wanted to impress her. That had always puzzled her. Why should he want to do that? Suddenly she had an idea, an idea that seemed to answer her question. She remembered that once when George called at the flat to take her out, she had been in the bath and Felicity had entertained George. That had been soon after Jan had started work and met George. Now Jan, eyes half closed, a frown wrinkling between her eyes, looked back. Knowing Felicity and her habit of dramatising everything and imagining the craziest stories, Jan found herself wondering if Felicity had strung a tale to George and given him the impression that they came from an influential and wealthy family. If so, that would explain George's sudden pressure of attention, the way he kept hovering over her desk, insisting they go out every evening, being very charming…

But if that was right, then it meant he had never loved her, and that hurt more than ever.

Had she loved him? How did you define love? she asked herself. She had *thought* she loved Frank, but then she had realised it was just that they knew one another so well, they felt at ease together. But that wasn't love.

Love should be thrilling, tempestuous, and heart-breaking as well as terribly exciting. You should feel breathless when you saw the man you loved, your knees should be like jelly, you should know that you would do anything – but anything – to make that man happy.

Had she felt like that about George? Closing her eyes, Jan tried to remember him and was startled to find how hard it was. He had been tall and thin with dark hair, rather too short, she had thought, dark eyes. He had to shave twice a day, which infuriated him. But lots of things infuriated him – a waiter's slowness, for instance, or if the wine was not *just* right. It could be an unexpected storm, even. She could remember thinking how edgy he was ... had she loved him? she asked herself again. Really loved him? Or was it the utter loneliness she had felt after telling Frank the truth? She remembered her shocked surprise when he agreed with her, kissed her affectionately and said it was better this way. Absurdly she had felt rejected. Then, coming out to a strange country where she had no friends, starting a new job, she had been first grateful for George's interest in her, then flattered by his attentions, and had somehow built up a romance that had never existed.

When George had asked questions about her family, she had told him the truth. Their father had died and her mother brought them up – also that she had a boutique in Lewes.

It was soon after that that George had quietly broken off their friendship. She should have recognised the truth at the time. George had never loved her, so she had never lost him. Nor was she at all sure she had ever loved him.

Then this strange happening. Suddenly she wondered if she had done the right thing. She went back carefully in her mind over Ludovic's unexpected call at her flat, his half-veiled threats to hamper Jarvis's fun, her gratitude to Jarvis for his kindness during those first awful days after George had jilted her – though, she thought, that was rather a melodramatic way of putting it. But she had been heartbroken and miserably alone, her mother over ten thousand miles away. Jarvis had been kind and understanding, so she had wanted to help him in return. But was this really helping him?

If only she could contact him. If she could write him a letter, and get an answer. But how could she do that here? Probably Ludovic had given Barry orders to look at any letters she wrote and to keep anything addressed to Jarvis.

Ludovic was determined to keep her away from Jarvis. How ironic it was, when she was the last person Jarvis would really want to see. They had liked one another but had little in common. It had merely been Jarvis's kindness of heart that had made him help her during those first bad days, nothing more, and in order to repay that kindness, she decided, she had done the right thing. Perhaps now Ludovic would leave Jarvis alone and give him a chance to live his own life.

CHAPTER THREE

Jan awoke early next day and from her bed she could see the lovely morning through the windows. It was too beautiful not to be enjoyed, she decided, so she showered, dressed and hurried out into the cool hall. Breakfast on the verandah would be very pleasant, she thought, but wondered how she could make Lucy understand.

Then as she passed the baize door, it opened. Jan stood still, surprised, also pleased, for it worried her to think of the Ryders who were so near yet so far away. It offended her sense of justice, for even if they did work for Ludovic, it shouldn't mean that they were to be treated as someone inferior.

A tall thin girl in a lilac nylon overall came into the hall. When she saw Jan, her hand flew to her mouth in dismay.

'I'm sorry,' she said.

Jan smiled, 'I'm not.' She went forward, holding out her hand. 'I've been wanting to meet you.'

The girl looked nervously over her shoulder and pulled the baize door to. 'Barry mustn't hear.'

'Why not?' Jan asked. 'I can't understand it. It doesn't make sense. I mean...'

'I know what you mean.'

The girl smiled. She was a pretty girl, but obviously the quiet type, Jan saw – in her mid-twenties, with soft honey-coloured hair tied back in a ponytail.

'I'm Esther Ryder,' the girl said, shaking Jan's hand and smiling. 'You see, Barry doesn't like us to get involved with the master's guests.'

'But I'm Mrs Fairlie's guest.'

Esther Ryder laughed. 'That makes it worse!'

'I just don't understand,' Jan repeated.

Esther shook her head. 'I know. It seems crazy, my word, it does. Actually it's mostly Barry's fault. Not fault, that's the wrong word, but he's a proud man and sensitive and he doesn't like being treated like a ... like a...' She looked round her as if searching for the right word.

'I know,' Jan said sympathetically.

'Well, in the past, things here have been difficult, at times. The master likes to be left completely alone. That's understandable, as he brings up a lot of work, then there's Mrs Fairlie…'

Jan nodded. 'Yes, please tell me about Mrs Fairlie.'

'You don't know her? You must have read about her in the papers and magazines.' Esther sounded almost shocked.

'I've only been in Australia a few months. Actually, as I said, she asked me up here and I just can't understand why she isn't here.'

Esther shrugged. 'She's probably forgotten she invited you. She's strange. Charming but vague. She's so busy do-gooding that she forgets everything and everyone else. You see,' she moved closer to Jan, looking again over her shoulder, 'Barry feels that … well that it's better if we don't get involved with, the Fairlie family. He's known Ludovic and worked for him for years. They're real buddies, but during working hours, Ludovic is the boss and Barry won't forget it. The same applies with Mrs Fairlie. He'd rather keep at a distance because she drives him mad with her vagueness and her complaints. She's a strange mixture.'

'What does she *do?*' Jan asked.

'What does she do? Oh, she's a real do-gooder. She goes all over Australia, and the world for that matter, lecturing and talking, on radio and T.V. about wild life preservation, cruelty to animals, bad housing, delinquent children.' Esther laughed. 'She can always find something to talk about and she loves it. I wish she wasn't like that, though. Life might be better for Jarvis and Sara.'

'Sara?' Jan asked.

'Jarvis's sister. She'll be along when the holidays come, but I doubt if her mum will.'

'I didn't know Jarvis had a sister.'

'They're not a close family, see. None of then care very much for one another. Seems to me there's only on person cares for them all and that's Ludovic. Barry says he's too good to them, that they should find their own way, but that's not like Ludovic. He has to help people.'

Somewhere in the house a door slammed. Esther looked startled.

'I must go. Don't tell Barry I've met you, please.'

'No, but I do wish...'

Esther smiled. 'So do I. Sometimes Barry goes off for a day or two and then ... okay?'

'Okay,' said Jan, and Esther opened the baize door and slipped through.

Jan went slowly out to sit on the verandah. She liked Esther and she liked Barry, and it would have been so nice if... Yet she could see Barry's point of view. Obviously Esther loved him very much and did what he wanted and not what she would like, but... Jan thought, looking at the beautiful scene before her, but when you love someone, wasn't that the natural thing to do?

Yet she was sorry she couldn't be friends with the Ryders, but at least now she would not feel so alone in the evenings because she had met Esther, Jan knew.

Quietly Lucy came to her side, handing her two magazines.

'Thank you,' Jan said, surprised. Then she realised Esther must have sent them, so she opened one magazine and looked down the Contents. She found a heading, 'Mrs Fairlie asks Why.'

It was a good article, brightly illustrated by photographs of a tall elegantly-dressed woman with fair hair, wearing an elaborate and fashionable blue hat that matched her suit. Jan read with interest:

'Always Mrs Fairlie asked WHY? *Why* can't the child feel more secure, why can't the wild birds be left in peace? Why ... why ... why? Mrs Fairlie must have raised thousands and thousands of dollars in her campaign to help those in need.'

Jan studied the photographs carefully. There was no resemblance at all to Jarvis, who had short darkish hair and a weak-looking chin. Esther had said a strange thing, Jan remembered, that if Mrs Fairlie did fewer do-good acts, it would be better for the children. Did that explain Jarvis's hatred of establishments and discipline, his revolt against rules, his refusal to conform as his uncle saw wise? Did Jarvis feel his mother didn't love him? Jan wondered.

One thing, Jan thought, Esther and Barry Ryder both obviously thought the world of Ludovic. That was just another side of his character. He was a strange man. Sometimes she longed for the weekend when he would appear, sometimes she dreaded it, afraid of the mood he might be in.

As Lucy brought out her breakfast on a tray, obviously having guessed Jan's desire to eat out on the verandah, Jan thought how much she looked forward every morning for her session with Rab.

He was so pleasant and relaxed; he could tease her without making her squirm, because she was happy with him, Jan realised. He was a kind man, just as Jarvis had been kind when she needed help.

She wondered how *he* was getting on with

his studies. She had not written to him, wondering if Ludovic would have told Barry to look at the letters, but she had written to Felicity and also to her mother several times, carefully avoiding any mention of the absence of her hostess.

Later Jane hurried down to the lagoon. As usual the morning flew by, for Jan enjoyed it all, especially as Rab was teaching her how to help him and not merely to stand and watch. This made it the more interesting, she realised. It was all so fascinating, such as the coral polyps which, Rab told her, were actually primitive animals.

He stood up, wiping the sweat from his face with the back of his hand, and smiling at her.

'Know something, Jan? For years, it was believed coral polyps were plants, but when the tide comes in they extend their tentacles to catch and poison the plankton and carry them to their mouths. Yet, when the tide is out, they shrink into stone houses.'

'Really, Rab?'

He nodded. 'We've learned so much and have so much to learn.'

Later he showed her clams. They were in their hundreds and when stared at through the clear water, they were the most incredibly amazing colours. Their mantles were electric blue or intensely green, sometimes yellow, mauve or orange. Often they were speckled.

'They've got the most amazing light-sensitive organs, Jan. These can detect the shadow of a man. Now watch.'

She followed him. As their shadows covered the clams, she heard the strange sound as the alarmed clams slammed shut. Water came spouting up in the air from their rapid movement.

Rab lifted his finger to his lips and signed to her to stay very still, so Jan obeyed. In a little while she saw the clams opening and their magnificent mantles slowly creeping out over the toothed edge of their valves.

'It's fantastic,' she said earnestly.

He smiled at her. 'It's amazing all the wonderful exciting things there are in the world, isn't it? I really think this holiday is doing you good, Jan. You look a different person already.'

She pulled a face and then smiled. 'Did I look so awful?'

He laughed. 'Not awful, Jan, but rather sad. You looked as if you had discovered that life is not always a bowl of cherries.'

She laughed. 'That's exactly how I felt. I'd

just been an absolute idiot.'

Then to her amazement she found herself able to talk to Rab as she could never have talked to Ludovic. She told Rab about Frank.

'We each needed someone and we chose one another because he lived next door. That wasn't really love, but it did shake me when I realised it was over and that, like me, Frank didn't know what real love was. Then we came out here and I met George.'

Rab listened silently, nodding here and there, and when Jan had finished, he smiled.

'Isn't that part of growing up, Jan? We all make mistakes we later regret and yet they help us, in the long run. Next time, Jan, you'll be more careful before you decide that it *is* love. It's so easy to be deceived. You're too sweet to be allowed to marry the wrong man, Jan, so just be very sure.'

He paused and she looked at him, for she had the feeling that he wanted to say more than he had already, but he merely smiled at her.

She laughed. 'If I go on feeling the way I do now, Rab, I'll never fall in love again.'

He laughed too. 'Famous last words,' he teased. 'Next thing, you'll be walking up the aisle while wedding bells ring.'

'I doubt it very much, Rab. Aren't the Fairlies funny people?' she went on. 'I just don't understand them.'

Rab collected his things.

'Don't try to work out what makes them tick, Jan. Wealthy people like that can't be normal. They think they're unique, that they can do what they like, regardless of other people, because they *know* they're right. I sometimes think it must be rather comforting to know you can't possibly make a mistake,' he laughed. 'On the other hand, I'd hate to wonder if every friend I made was only after my money.'

He stood up, laden with his things.

'Time you went up for lunch, Jan. See you tomorrow.'

'Of course.'

She waited as Rab walked over the wet sand and then on to the jetty and his small cabin cruiser. He lifted a hand in farewell and she watched the snowy crest of water that followed the boat as it sped out of the lagoon into the open sea. She walked back to the house slowly, hardly noticing the sleeping bats or hearing the birds as they sang and rustled in the leaves. She had so much to think about.

Was Rab right? Was life more difficult for Ludovic because of his money? Had he been born with the idea that he was always right? Yet Esther had said how good he was to the children. Jarvis and Sara, Jan thought, wondering why Jarvis had never mentioned Sara. How old would Sara be and where was she? Questions seemed to be coming faster and faster, she thought. Why hadn't their mother done enough for them? as Esther implied.

As the days passed and the weekend approached, Jan's mind was like a confused muddle. She wrote to her mother about the beauty of the place, but not about the quiet loneliness that she had at first seen as solitary confinement, but now as a time to think, relax and dream.

Jan could *not* tell her mother that she was lonely, nor that the long dark quiet evenings when everything was so still were what she hated, nor describe how often she sat, wishing there could be the creak of a floorboard or the closing of a door, just something to show there was life, in the quiet house. How well built it must be, she thought, for never a sound came from the Ryders' part of the house. No one locked doors at night, since there was no one on the island who would steal. The lights blazed away until midnight when they all, except a few, were automatically dimmed.

So all Jan could write about was the beauty of it, the rest she was having, how well she felt.

Meanwhile her mind was going round and round in circles, thinking about Jarvis, Felicity, who had never written, also about Rab and the Ryders, but always she ended up by thinking about Ludovic.

As Rab had once said, he often wondered what made Ludovic tick. She wondered too. How was it he could be so different? A sort of Jekyll and Hyde, Jan thought with a smile, as she imagined Ludovic's expression if she told him that.

On Friday, Ludovic arrived and dropped a pile of things on the verandah by her side, such as snorkels, face-masks, frogmen's flippers, surface and even an underwater camera with a tripod.

'It's the gear I promised you,' he told her, when he returned from his shower and joined her for tea. 'How goes it, Jan? Not too bored?'

She stared at him. Each time he came up, she found herself doing just that, waiting with an uneasy squeamish feeling to find out what mood he was in. Today it seemed like one of his good relaxed moods, so she smiled.

'Most certainly not. Rab's teaching me a lot.'

For a moment it was as if a shadow passed over Ludovic's face.

'I'm glad of that.'

'How's Sydney looking?' she asked.

'Just as usual, terribly hot, crowded and noisy. It's a joy to come up here.'

'Ludovic,' she said slowly, 'when's your … your sister-in-law coming here?'

He stretched his long legs, then picking up his cup of tea, he looked at her.

'Impatient to see her? Eager to get the inquisition over?' he asked, smiling, but there was a strange cold look in his eyes.

'No, it's just … just…' She hesitated, not wanting to say anything that might change his mood.

To her surprise he smiled.

'Well, let's just forget it. Tomorrow I'll introduce you to underwater swimming. Okay with you?'

She felt herself relax, and smiled as she said:

'I can't wait to learn. It sounds too thrilling for words.'

He nodded. 'I love it. I think you will too.'

The next day proved how right he was. He was patience itself, for, at first, she was slow at learning. Then, as she learned how to do what he told her, she found this new world utterly enchanting. Her limbs hardly moved, waving as the astronauts' feet had waved on the moon.

She swam by Ludovic's side, admiring the fascinating little fish and the vividly coloured coral polyps. He showed her small caves, explaining everything. As she floated through the water, the long dark tentacles of an octopus moved towards her. Instinctively she turned to Ludovic and immediately he was by her side, his arm round her. The panic that had turned her legs to lumps of iron and her heart pounding frantically vanished as she saw she had been frightened by a shadow!

Later she laughed, but Ludovic was sympathetic.

'Things like that can be frightening,' he said.

Afterwards they lay in the sun. Gone completely was that stern arrogant mask of the city Ludovic, Jan saw as she stared at him, lying by her side, his eyes shut, then he opened his eyes and smiled:

'Well, do I make the grade?'

Her cheeks burned. 'I'm sorry, I didn't mean to stare.'

He laughed. 'I don't mind. I'm used to it.'

'I suppose...' She paused and tried again. 'I suppose you've got lots of girl-friends.'

'Masses of them,' he laughed. 'I've lost count. Why?'

'Well, I...'

She sat up, really flustered. What was the answer to that? she wondered. She looked down the sands to the palm trees as they stood, bent against the ocean wind, their fronds moving.

'Well?' he said impatiently.

'I ... I just wondered.'

It sounded lame, but she could think of nothing better.

'It would be strange if I didn't,' he said, his voice bitter.

Jan was startled by his stark arrogance.

'Why should it be strange?' she asked him, her courage renewed by her quick anger. 'You're not all that handsome. You might be to some girls, but you're not everyone's choice...'

Even as she said it, she regretted the words. It was not necessary to be rude! Indeed, it was childish of her.

But instead of being angry, he looked amused.

'My dear child, when will you grow up? It's not my handsome looks or my undoubted charm that makes the girls swarm round me. It's my money.'

There was a bitterness again in his voice as she stared at him, and she wondered if that was one of the things that made him tick. The fact that he could trust no one because of his cynicism. Because he believed he would be loved only for his money. How awful it must be to feel like that, Jan thought, startled by the idea. How terrible never to know if anyone loved you for yourself.

He began to stand up, deftly unfolding his long legs.

'By the way, Jan, I'm going deep-water fishing tomorrow with Barry. Like to come along?'

She hesitated for a moment. Deep-water fishing? Was she a good enough sailor? She would hate to be sick in front of Ludovic, and then she thought of the long lonely week ahead, the fact that soon Ludovic would be gone again, flying back to Sydney.

'I'd love to,' she said.

Ludovic smiled. 'Somehow I thought you

would. I'll tell Lucy to call you early. By the way,' he added as they collected their things and began to walk home through the woods. 'I'm afraid I've got to be unsociable tonight, as I've brought a lot of work with me. You won't be lonely?'

'Of course not,' she said quickly. 'I'm used to it. In a way, I'm beginning to love it.'

Barry Ryder and two of the aboriginal men, whom Jan had often seen working on the island, went with them in the forty-foot launch.

Jan was surprised as she heard Barry greet Ludovic in a friendly way:

'Everything's beaut, Lud. Good luck!'

It startled Jan, as it was such a different reaction from Barry's usual polite, formal attitude.

Ludovic, in grey shorts, a brown shirt and matching peaked cap, grinned in reply.

'I've brought my mascot along.' He gestured with his hand towards Jan. 'Only hope she doesn't prove to be a jinx!'

Both men laughed.

'Good thing she isn't a redhead,' Barry said, and smiled at Jan. Even his smile was different here, she noticed, friendly. The mask of formality had vanished.

113

'Done any deep sea fishing before?' he asked.

'No, this is my first time,' she admitted.

'It's exciting, but can be boring.'

'Luckily Jan isn't easily bored,' Ludovic joined in. 'Better get going, Barry.'

'Okay.'

Barry left them and soon the boat began to throb with noise, then shot forward through the calm blue water of the lagoon.

Ludovic leant over the rail by Jan's side and the silence seemed to go on for ever.

'What sort of fish are you going to catch?' Jan asked, uncomfortable in the silence, yet a little worried about breaking it.

Ludovic turned to her at once.

'Barracuda, black marlin, sword-fish … maybe even a thresher shark,' he said, his voice casual. 'Depends on the luck.'

Later he told her more.

'We shall just drift along and wait for the fish to bite.'

The boat still went through the water fast, spray coming up to salt Jan's face. She felt in the way and tried to look inconspicuous, but the two men paid her little attention, as they were busy preparing for the fight.

When she saw what they were doing, she felt sick, for Barry held an eighteen-inch fish in his hand which was struggling wildly to break away, as he thrust the hook into it and then tossed it into the water.

'Barry!' she cried out impulsively. 'He was alive. You can't do that!'

Her voice sounded loud in the quietness, no longer broken by the roar of the motor, for it had been slowed down and they were more or less drifting through the water. Both men stopped what they were doing and stared at her.

'Why on earth not?' Ludovic asked.

Her hand went to her mouth, for she felt horribly sick, but tried to make him understand.

'Live bait. What a terribly cruel idea! That poor fish, with the hook in his mouth, being pulled through the water, knowing he's going to be caught by a ... a...'

Ludovic looked amused, balancing as the boat suddenly rolled.

'My dear child, that fish is free to swim where he likes. If he's clever enough he can elude the shark.'

'But not for ever,' she put in. 'He's on your line, so he can't really get away.'

'He wouldn't get away anyhow. If the shark didn't get him, we would, and probably eat him for supper.' The two men were

115

openly laughing. 'Look, Jan,' Ludovic went on, 'I didn't know you were squeamish. Go down below to the cabin and you needn't watch. I can't see what you're making such a fuss about.'

'Can't you see that it's torture? That poor fish, knowing the shark is coming after him. It'd be kinder to kill him outright.'

'But then I wouldn't get my shark,' Ludovic pointed out, still smiling.

'Why have you to get a shark?' Jan was on her feet, eyes blazing, cheeks red. 'Why? Simply because you have to show how strong you are – because you want people to think you're so wonderful. Well, I, for one, don't. I think you're cruel and … and hateful!'

She turned, half-stumbling down the steps to the cabin, sank on to the couch and covered her face. She was so angry … and yet sorry she'd said those things. Yet it was true. He was cruel – cruel to everyone.

It was no good. He was hateful. Just because he was so rich, it didn't give him the right to trample on everyone.

She seemed to be sitting in the cabin for hours, but nothing would make her go on deck to witness what she felt was horrible. Once Barry came down to the small galley, gave her a cup of coffee and some biscuits and grinned.

'Burned out yet?' he asked.

She looked at him, refusing to smile. Then felt ashamed of herself, for it wasn't his fault, it was all Ludovic's. So she smiled.

'I don't understand.'

'Lud said you had a quick temper but it soon burned itself out. Come up when I shout and you'll really see something,' he promised. 'So far nothing's bitten.'

'So I'm a jinx!'

He grinned.

'Jinx? Little wildcat, I'd say. You sure did blow up at him. Not many girls do.'

'I'm not many girls,' she said slowly.

He leant on the table, his face suddenly grave.

'Look, I know he makes one mad at times, but it's just his way.'

'Is it?' Jan allowed herself to be sarcastic. 'I suppose beneath that unpleasant exterior there burns a golden heart.'

She saw the smile playing round Barry's mouth, but he answered gravely.

'Matter of fact, there does. I wouldn't have this good job but for that fact. Look, try to see this fishing game from the right angle. When the shark catches the fish, it's over in a few moments. The fish doesn't know he's being chased by a shark – he simply can't understand why he can't get right away from the boat. Fish don't have brains.'

'How do we know?'

Barry straightened, shook his head, his face a mixture of exasperation and amusement.

'He's quite right, my word he is! It's just no good trying to talk sense to you once you get mad. I'm wasting my time. Come up all the same when you hear us shouting. The fish, poor wee soul...' He grinned. 'An unintended pun, for it happens to be a Kahawai fish. Anyhow, the fish'll be dead, so you needn't feel upset. There'll be a battle, a real battle.'

'I hope he loses – and I don't mean the fish,' said Jan, turning her head away, but not before she saw the grin on Barry's face.

He left her alone and she wished she hadn't said those things. He was probably repeating them to Ludovic and they were both enjoying a good laugh at her expense.

She sat on and time crept by. It was close and hot in the cabin and she longed for the fresh wind on deck. But her pride wouldn't let her go. Then she began to think over what Barry said. She asked herself whether she had been ridiculous to worry about the fish. It could be said that it was a better death to be quickly swallowed by a shark than to lie panting and puffing on deck, waiting for the mercy of a knife.

Suddenly she heard someone shout excitedly and before she realised what she was doing, she was up the stairs and on deck clinging to the rail, looking at Ludovic strapped in his chair, leaning forward as the line went screaming off the reel. Jan's eyes followed it and saw the enormous black fish suddenly arch into the air as he leapt and then crashed back into the sea.

She gasped, for that enormous body had seemed to shut out the sky as it hung, suspended for a second in the air. Neither of the men seemed to notice her. Barry was putting some canvas harness on Ludovic, then clipping it to the rail. Ludovic was leaning forward, his face intent.

She had no idea how long it lasted. She stood quietly, clinging to the railing, watching Ludovic as he tried to reel in the huge fish. Ludovic braced his legs one moment, pulled back into the chair as far as he could, then bent forward, reeling in whatever line he could. The next moment she would hear the screaming of the reel as the fish got away.

Some of the excitement of the fight filled Jan's veins. She found her hands clenched, but she managed to stifle the shout of encouragement in her throat. No one talked. There was an air of tension as everyone save the aboriginal at the wheel watched Ludovic at work.

His face was set like a mask. No smile. No life. Just set, his mouth a thin line. He looked tired, Jan thought, glancing at her wrist watch and realising with a shock just how long the fight had been going on.

The fish seemed to be dashing ahead and, although the engine was running and she knew that the fish wasn't towing them, she realised they had to follow his course, and a crazy course it was, loops, twisting, turning, zigzags and even figures of eight as if the fish was laughing at them.

Then quite suddenly it looked as if Ludovic was winning, for the huge fish stopped racing and moved gently through the water, allowing Ludovic to reel him in and Jan, watching, thought quickly: 'So you've won again!' She wasn't sure if she was glad or sorry. Glad or sorry that Ludovic had, as usual, won his battle? But she was sorry that the great gallant fish had been caught.

And then everything happened so swiftly

that she was never quite able to describe the scene afterwards. The fish must have been playing a diabolically diplomatic game, for without warning from his gentle roll, he suddenly shot forward, rushing off into the opposite direction. The rod was pulled forward and Ludovic with it … but the fighting harness held him, dragging him with the chair over the side of the boat into the water.

Barry and the abos acted fast, but Jan's hands were against her mouth as she stifled a scream and she felt absurdly weak as she saw them haul Ludovic aboard and help him out of the tightly strapped harness.

It was then he looked at her. He must have seen her wide frightened eyes, her white face, for he nodded reassuringly.

'Everything's okay, Jan. It often happens. He was too clever for me.'

She swallowed.

'I thought … I thought he'd eat you.'

He laughed.

'Take more than a shark to eat me, Jan! Man, am I wet! I'll slip down and put on something dry.'

He left them while Barry tidied up and occasionally glanced at Jan, who had sat down, her hands clasped, face still white, as she stared into the distance.

'He's right, you know,' Barry said as he walked past her. 'It often happens.'

'But he could have been killed,' she said, the words having to be dragged out of her.

'That's one of the chances,' Barry said lightly. 'We're used to them.'

'I … I…'

Suddenly she knew she was going to be sick. She turned to lean over the side of the boat, her whole body shuddering.

An arm went round her and then a glass was held to her lips. The liquid burned her throat and made her cough, but the warmth inside her seemed to bring her back from the dark abyss into which she had dived for a moment.

'Okay?'

It was Ludovic's voice. She opened her eyes and stared at him. He had pulled on an old jacket and some shorts, but his hair was wet.

'That's no way to behave,' he scolded, but gently.

She swallowed.

'I'm sorry, it's just… I'm sorry, I'm being a jinx, aren't I? I mean, you lost the fish and … and nearly lost your life.'

'Aren't you glad I lost the shark?' he asked,

the gentleness leaving his voice. 'You must be delighted that I lost.'

She swallowed again and shivered. His arm tightened round her and he made her take another drink.

'No,' she said, 'I'm sorry you lost it, but I'm glad the shark got away.'

He smiled.

'So am I. It deserved to, because it put up a good fight, no holds barred. Come on below to the cabin. You need a strong cup of tea and something to eat. Coming, Barry?'

'Coming, Lud!' Barry shouted.

Jan felt absurdly unsteady, but Ludovic helped her down the stairs and the two men fussed over her, making the tea, unpacking the delicious sandwiches, talking to one another, but bringing Jan into the conversation, making her laugh, until the colour returned to her pale cheeks.

Later they went on deck as the sun began to go down and the sky was an incredibly beautiful sight. The island appeared out of the mist and, when they moored at the jetty, Barry had all the clobber ready to be carried ashore.

As they stopped, his manner changed. When he spoke to Ludovic, he called him 'sir' and he spoke formally to 'Miss Shaw' just as though those hours of friendliness had never been.

Jan walked back to the house by Ludovic's side, and mentioned this.

'Why is Barry so different out at sea?' she asked, and tried to explain what she had noticed.

Ludovic, walking slowly by her side, smiled.

'Well, when we're on a project like that we're buddies. Mates. See what I mean? Equals. So I'm "Lud" to him. Once we land, I'm boss, so I'm "sir" or the master. Does that make sense? Look at it this way. I get on pretty well with all my staff.' He smiled wryly. 'Shall I say, most of my staff, that is. Now if we were all on Christian name terms, it does make it a bit muddly. My secretary would come into the room. Hi, Ludovic, she'd say, Mark and Tommy want to talk to you, and the two directors would come in and thank Laetitia for introducing them. See what I mean? It just wouldn't work.'

'Yes, I do see,' she agreed.

The light was falling fast – the sun a blaze of red, just about to drop out of sight on the horizon. Ludovic hurried his pace a little and Jan had almost to run to keep up with him.

'You did mind losing that shark, didn't

you?' she asked abruptly.

Ludovic glanced down.

'Of course I did. Any fisherman would.'

'No, it meant more to you than that. Ludovic, why do you have to dominate everyone?' she asked earnestly. 'I mean, when you're around, all the other men seem to fade away.'

'They do?' He sounded startled.

'Yes. I don't know why, but they all seem to get shorter and to look ... well, insignificant.' She looked up at him. 'Were you bullied as a small boy by your big brother, Ludovic? I mean, it could be a sort of inferiority complex, couldn't it?'

His shout of laughter seemed to echo through the woods and it disturbed hundreds of small creatures, for suddenly the trees were alive with noise and fluttering wings.

'Me – an inferiority complex!' Ludovic was choking with laughter. 'One thing about you, Jan,' he said, as they came out into the open and the house was before them, a blaze of light, 'you do make me laugh.'

As they went inside, she wondered if that was a compliment. Somehow she didn't think it was. Then she remembered Jarvis and the letter she wanted to write to him.

'Ludovic...' She realised her voice had changed, become pleading, but it was too late to alter it. 'I'd like to do some shopping. Could I...'

'Of course. Barry goes ashore every other day. Just tell him you want to go. I'll be seeing him later today and I'll tell him. You can go as often as you like. You're not a prisoner, you know.'

They were standing in the tall cool hall and Jan looked up at him.

'Aren't I?'

He put his hands on her shoulders. 'No, you are not. You're perfectly free. You can go back to Sydney whenever you like.'

She hesitated. 'And Jarvis?'

Ludovic smiled. 'You know very well that Jarvis's future is in your hands.'

'Just one more thing,' she said quickly. 'When will Mrs Fairlie be here?'

'In her own good time. She got held up. This often happens, you know. You can't hurry her. Are you unhappy here? I got the impression you liked the place. Do you want to go back to your scruffy little flat?'

She felt the colour rise in her cheeks. 'It wasn't...' she began quickly.

He stooped and lightly kissed her on the cheek.

'Thank you for making us laugh so much. I'm sure you've done Barry and me more good than all the tonics in the world,' he said, and left her. 'See you later at dinner.'

She stood still and watched him go to his room, then turned into her own. After dinner the long empty week would stretch ahead. And then she remembered something and her depression vanished. At least, she could write to Jarvis, and go to the mainland.

That evening after dinner they sat outside on the screened verandah, having coffee.

'You didn't bring any work with you this time?' Jan asked, as she looked at the gorgeous molten silver of the moonlight on the lagoon. 'You're usually so busy.'

He was stretched out in a long wicker chair.

'It struck me that even I need a holiday sometimes. I feel so completely relaxed here. Has it the same effect on you?'

Jan straightened the front of her yellow silk frock. She had done up her long dark hair on top of her head elaborately.

'Yes. It's a strange, difficult-to-explain feeling – at least to me.' She glanced at him. There was little lighting, so she could hardly see his face, but the sternness seemed to have gone, at least temporarily. 'It's unreal, almost as if it's too good to be true. The outside world no longer matters. I live from day to day, just enjoying each day.'

'You make it sound like Utopia, but I know what you mean. I think that's what I like about the island. It's so different from the rat race in Sydney.'

'Lewes, where I come from, is quite small, but even there the traffic is growing all the time and there's such a noise as you walk along the pavements you have to shout and...'

'Here it's so quiet you can almost hear yourself breathe,' he agreed.

'Yes,' she said simply, and leant back in her chair, content and strangely happy.

Her mind went briefly to George whom she had thought she loved so much. Now she mentally thanked God for having ended that so-called romance, for that was all it had been. It had just been wishful thinking born of loneliness, and the blank left in her life because she no longer loved Frank, her childhood love.

Now she was completely relaxed, her head against a deep red pillow, her eyes half closed.

And then Ludovic spoke. His voice had changed, sounded amused.

'Know something, Jan?' he began casually. 'You've rather disappointed me. When I first met you, I was impressed by your sincerity. I knew you would always tell me the truth. Now I realise you're as much of a hypocrite as the rest of us.'

Jan felt her body stiffen. Her mouth was dry and for a moment she found it hard to breathe, wondering if he had found out the truth – that she was not Jarvis's beloved but his beloved's sister. She gave a tiny shiver. Well, she had always known that this moment must come, but it had come sooner than she had expected and had caught her unawares. The only thing was to face him, to be truthful and tell him *why* she had helped Jarvis, because she was grateful to him, because she believed that Ludovic, his uncle, was treating him badly, absurdly for this day and age. Slowly the anger seemed to creep through her veins. Ludovic had no right to be so domineering, so arrogant, so sure he was right when he arranged other people's lives. Jarvis was no child. He was twenty and fully entitled to know who he liked and to be left in peace to pass his exams his own way.

Jan opened her mouth to start the attack

when Ludovic spoke, and what he said silenced her completely, it was so unexpected.

'You're a mass of contradictions, Jan. You're not consistent. You eat meat. You eat fish. You've never expressed any distress or even inquisitiveness as to how they die. Yet you create a scene like an hysterically neurotic old maid just because we use live bait.' His voice was sarcastic. 'Poor little fish, you say, you can't do that to him. What do you think happens before you eat roast chicken? Does the cockerel enjoy being caught and killed? Of course it doesn't.'

He paused. Jan realised that, looked at that way, of course, he was right. If she really minded about how animals, fish and birds were slaughtered, she should be a vegetarian.

'Another strange thing about you, Jan,' Ludovic continued, 'is, as I said, your inconsistency. You rush below to the cabin because you can't bear the sight, yet the instant I caught the shark you were there, almost screaming away, as excited as we were. You reminded me of a Roman watching the Christians being thrown to the lions, or, perhaps more appropriately, a French revolutionary sitting and knitting as the heads of the hated aristocracy fell. You did enjoy the fight, didn't you?'

Jan nodded. She spread out her fingers on her skirt and stared at them.

'I guess you're right, Ludovic. It was just … just that I couldn't bear to see the poor fish wriggling in Barry's hand, trying to get free and then … then that horrible hook in his mouth…'

'In other words, you're squeamish when you actually *see* things happen, but so long as you don't see, it doesn't matter.'

Jan jumped to her feet, scraping her chair noisily.

'Yes, you're right. But there was a difference in the … the live fish and the shark. I knew the shark was powerful, much stronger than you, so you didn't have…'

'All the odds on my side?' he finished for her. 'I see. That was a battle, eh?'

'It certainly was. You must be terribly strong.'

Ludovic laughed.

'You have to be to survive. That shark was a wily brute. He deserved to escape. By the way, Jan…' His face had altered; now he leaned forward and she saw the way his eyes had narrowed, his eyebrows almost meeting. 'I must ask you not to be so insulting in front of my staff.'

Jan's cheeks burned.

'I'm … I'm sorry. It was rude of me.'

'The understatement of the year, I'd say. It was childish, completely uncalled-for. Fortunately it was only Barry with me and he understood. I would point out that you are my guest...'

'Unwillingly,' she said quickly.

He stood up, and she wished she hadn't said that word, for it seemed to have provoked him. He came and stood by her side and as she moved back he followed her, quietly, unostentatiously, but at last she had retreated so much that her back was against the wall of the house and he stood close in front of her.

'Unwillingly?' he repeated. 'Yet you told me you were happy here, that you loved it. Are you a liar?'

It was absurd, but she was afraid. She told herself not to be stupid. Ludovic wasn't the type of man to hurt a woman. But was her assumption correct?

'I am happy here... I wasn't lying,' she said breathlessly. 'But you must admit you … you gave me little choice. I mean, if I hadn't come...'

'It would have been tough on Jarvis?'

132

Ludovic's voice sounded amused, now, rather than angry. 'Poor delicate Jarvis! How protected he must feel. All you girls rushing to look after him. So you were forced to come here, against your will and, perhaps, your better judgement, simply because you wanted to protect my nephew.'

'You made it very plain what would happen if I didn't.'

He stood back and smiled.

'I'm glad you had the sense to recognise that. One day Jarvis will thank you.'

He walked out of the verandah, letting the door swing to behind him.

The next day after lunch she wrote to Jarvis. She was not sure if she should be frank with him and say bluntly that she had been morally blackmailed by his uncle and forced to come here or else Jarvis would have been affected by it, for she did not put it past Ludovic to have someone keeping an eye on Jarvis's mail. Suppose she wrote that and Ludovic read it?

So very carefully she chose her words and hoped Jarvis would be able to read between the lines.

'Dear Jarvis,' she began, 'I find it difficult to believe, but I've been told that since you met me you've stopped working at your studies. Apparently I've distracted you. I'm sure this is pure imagination on your mother's part, but she's afraid you'll fail your Finals if I'm around. She kindly asked me to stay here, but so far she hasn't turned up. I'm very happy here but wanted to let you know why I suddenly disappeared, in case you wondered. Felicity should be coming back soon, but I haven't heard from her although I've written. Good luck with your exams. Yours… she finished, and signed her name with a flourish.

She was sure Jarvis would burst out laughing when he read it and mentally thank her for backing up his crazy scheme, but did he really think he could fool his uncle indefinitely? she wondered. What would happen when Felicity returned and she and Jarvis started going everywhere together? It was also on the cards that Felicity would be invited up here, which could cause complications.

Jan addressed the envelope, sealed it and put it in her handbag. She also wrote to Iris telling her how beautiful the island was.

In the morning as she 'fossicked' with Rab, she told him about the scene on the boat. He laughed and yet sympathised.

'I know. I hate live bait, too. Yet I'm inconsistent, because I'm always killing specimens to study them. You know, Jan, life isn't as straightforward as one would like it to be. Was it a good fight with the shark?'

'Absolutely super!' Jan had clasped her hands as she remembered. 'Ludovic was so strong, so determined, but the shark was just as clever. He had Ludovic fooled.'

'And you were glad?'

She coloured.

'Yes – until Ludovic was jerked into the water. Then I was really scared. I thought the shark might eat him.'

Rab had laughed. 'It 'ud take more than a shark to conquer him. I reckon that one day a woman will.'

'A woman?' Jan was startled. 'You think Ludovic would let a woman...'

Rab laughed again. 'Not eat him.'

'Rab, you're out of your mind!' Jan had begun to laugh. 'Ludovic would never let a woman rule him. Why, he has to be the big noise, the boss...'

Rab had stopped working and stood up, taking off the protective gloves, rubbing his hands together.

'He has to *think* he is. Know something, Jan? It's these big strong arrogant men who have the most vulnerable Achilles' heel.'

135

'Achilles' heel?'

Rab nodded.

'Yes, each one of us has a weakness. Mine? Tearful sad eyes. Just let anyone gaze at me like a spaniel and I'm sunk. They can call the tune.'

'I can't see anyone calling the tune to Ludovic. He'd never let them, he'd never accept it. He's just not like that,' Jan had told him.

Rab had chuckled. 'But you see, he won't know.'

'He won't know?' She was puzzled.

'My dear Jan, a clever woman could manage Ludovic as easy as … as I handle this crowbar.' He pointed at the heavy crowbar he often had to use to loosen the coral. 'She'll know how to manipulate him and yet let him think he's still the Big Noise. It's always happening. In the past many of the kings were actually puppets in women's hands. The women were clever enough to keep in the background, but they did the ruling, all right.'

'Maybe, Rab, but I can't imagine Ludovic letting…'

'That's the whole point, Jan. He won't *let* her because he won't know he's letting her. He'll love her so much he'll do everything she wants without his realising it.'

Jan had stared, puzzled, at Rab.

'Do you really think that?'

'I do. Most certainly I do. It's these so-called tough guys who, when they fall in love, really fall in love. Just let some lovely clever girl come along and Ludovic will be jelly in her hands.'

'I can't imagine it...' Jan had persisted.

Rab had laughed and begun to collect his things, for it was nearly lunch time.

'Neither can I, to be honest, Jan. She'd have to be clever as well as beautiful. Maybe one day she'll come along.'

That evening Jan found herself remembering their conversation. She sat alone on the screened verandah, listening to the quietness, the occasional thud as a coconut fell to the ground. Suddenly the low persistent humming of cicadas began. That sound, plus the sight of the palm trees silhouetted against the dark sky yet easily seen because of the moonlight, seemed to prove the magic of this tropical island. Ludovic had described it as Utopia. She wondered whether Rab was right in his theories. Would Ludovic one day meet a clever girl who would twist him round her little finger without his knowing it?

Next morning Jan was ready – when the carriage with the two beautiful black horses arrived to take her for the first part of her journey. She felt absurdly excited about it, yet the island had never felt like a prison, she told herself. Or was it the letter to Jarvis that thrilled her so much, for although she was having a wonderful holiday, she hated the guilty feeling she had had when she thought Ludovic had found out the truth – that it was Felicity Jarvis loved, not Jan!

The horses trotted with solemn grace along the earth road and she sat back, feeling rather absurd as though she had been transformed to another world or era. She looked affectionately at the island's mountain which had become a familiar friend; indeed, she realised how fond she had grown of the island, not only for the fascinating beauty of it, but because for her it had become home. A strange feeling, one she couldn't understand, she thought.

Barry was waiting by the boat. He welcomed her with a smile. As he helped her on board, he said, 'I'd like you to meet my wife.'

Jan was so surprised she nearly tripped over, but recovered her balance and smiled up at him. 'I'd love to meet her.'

'Esther!' he called, and Jan watched as the quiet pretty girl came out of the small cabin. 'I want you to meet my wife, Miss Shaw. Esther, this is Miss Shaw.'

The two girls solemnly shook hands, Jan trying not to laugh but knowing she must not reveal that they had already met.

'The master,' Barry went on, 'thought it would be more enjoyable for you if you had someone of your own sex with you.'

'Ludovic?' Jan was startled, then she thought she understood. He didn't trust her and Esther was just a spy! Suddenly Jan wanted to laugh. Just how melodramatic could she get? she asked herself. Ludovic was always accusing her of making drama out of nothing, and it looked as if he was right.

The two girls stood together but near Barry; they hardly spoke, but looked at one another meaningly every now and then. Jan had chosen a white dress, but Esther was wearing dark green slacks and a cream blouse. Now, as they stood almost silently, they gazed ahead as the boat raced towards the nearest island. The water was calm, with few rollers, and that reminded Jan that at least she had not been seasick the day before.

'I hear you went fishing,' Esther said, her voice cautious, glancing at Barry as she spoke. 'How brave of you. I'm always sea-sick.'

Jan turned at once, glad that the silence had been broken.

'Quite frankly, that was what I was scared of, too. Luckily I wasn't.' She looked at Barry who was staring ahead, as if he could not hear what they said. 'Did ... did your husband tell of the fuss I made?'

Esther chuckled. 'Yes. He admired you for your courage, didn't you, darling?' She put her hand on her husband's arm.

He turned to smile at her and then at Jan.

'It takes guts to stand up to the master, and you've got lots.'

Jan blushed. 'I don't think it was that – I felt sick and ... well...' she laughed a little, 'almost hysterical, but I was really scared when Ludovic fell overboard.'

'He's used to that,' Barry told her with a smile. 'It's part of the fun.'

'Sooner you than me, Barry,' Jan said, laughing.

'Me too,' Esther breathed.

The whole atmosphere had changed. Now Jan found she could chatter away to both Barry and Esther without feeling anxious

140

lest she involve Esther in some trouble. Was it because Ludovic had asked Barry to take Esther along? If so, Jan thought, she was grateful to him.

Sometimes it worried her to think how much she should be grateful to Ludovic for. After all, this was a wonderful holiday he was giving her and he need not have gone out of his way to entertain her at the weekends, as he had done. Yet somehow, Jan thought, she knew it would be difficult to thank him, and to meet that amused, patronising smile, for he would be sure to ask:

'What for?'

They came closer to an island. Esther, talking naturally now, told her it was the nearest island and just a small town.

'Of course, it's packed during the season. I often come over with Barry, so you must tell us whenever you'd like to come. It makes a change and...' she looked at Barry with a smile, 'gives us a chance to see people.'

'I'm afraid Esther finds it rather too quiet at times,' Barry said. 'Do you, Miss Shaw?'

Jan hesitated. She had the uncomfortable feeling that anything she said might be reported back to Ludovic.

'Not during the day, but the evenings seem so long,' she admitted. 'I've always lived with a family or a friend and...'

Esther nodded. 'When Sara comes she'll be good company.'

Barry snorted. 'Throwing tantrums and showing off!'

'Barry darling!' Esther looked at him. 'Can you blame her?'

He frowned and turned away, his voice curt as he said they would be there in a short while, as he weaved his way into the lagoon and they passed the yachts rolling gently in the quiet swell, and the small cabin cruisers.

Esther's cheeks were bright red and Jan quickly looked at the quay they were approaching. Poor Esther, she had put her foot in it, Jan realised, Barry was annoyed, for everything about the master was perfect, that was obvious, so no criticism must be made.

Once ashore, Esther and Jan separated from Barry, who had business to do. They all arranged to meet in an hour. Together they walked along the shingle road which was lined on either side with tourist-inviting shops.

'I want to buy some frocks, drip-dry, of course,' Jan said casually.

'You must find it terribly hot,' said Esther.

She still sounded a little unhappy so Jan turned to her impulsively.

'Esther, you didn't say *anything*. I mean, anything wrong.'

Esther's eyes were miserable.

'I know, but I did hint. You see, Ludovic has been so wonderful to Barry and to me, too, that Barry gets furious if I ... all the same,' her unhappy face changed and she nodded, her mouth a thin line, 'all the same, you'll see for yourself, Jan, what a rotten mother Mrs Fairlie is. She's no relation of Ludovic's, so I don't see why...' Her voice was unsteady for a moment. 'Barry's like that, though. Ludovic means so much to him, and I do understand why.'

'This was Ludovic's idea? I mean about you coming with me?' Jan asked.

Esther nodded.

'He told Barry you wanted to go to the mainland, as we nickname the island, and I think Barry must have frowned, because he hates taking Ludovic's visitors ashore as they never turn up at the right time and Barry is a stickler for punctuality so it makes him mad and, of course, he can't say anything. Well, maybe Ludovic saw the frown, for he was smiling as he looked at me and asked me if I'd mind meeting you and showing you the other island.'

'And Barry? What did he say?'

'He seemed to like the idea. He likes you, you know.'

Jan's cheeks were hot. 'I'm glad. I like him,' she smiled, 'and you.'

Esther laughed. 'Well, we must play it cool and not expect everything to change overnight, but when Sara comes Barry doesn't mind what I do for her, and I think, in time, it'll be the same with you.'

Pausing outside a bow-windowed shop, Jan stared at the frocks on show, but she was thinking fast. What was it Esther had said – *in time,* it'll be the same with you.'

In time? What did that mean? How much longer would Ludovic expect her to stay on the island?

'I like that one,' Esther said, breaking into Jan's thoughts and pointing to an orange-coloured frock with loose chiffon sleeves. 'You'd look smashing in it.'

Twenty minutes and four frocks later, they left the shop and Jan remembered something.

'Where's the post office?' she asked. 'I brought some letters with me to post.'

Esther led the way to a small shop-cum-post office. Jan bought some stamps and then dropped the letters in the box. Outside in the sunshine she smiled at Esther.

'Is there time for a cold drink or something?'

Esther looked at her wrist watch.

'Oh yes. There's a nice café near the quay and if Barry sees us sitting there, he might join us.' She smiled at Jan. 'I have enjoyed this,' she added.

Jan smiled back. 'So have I.'

'Well,' said Esther, 'let's not push our luck, but I'll see what I can do. You play canasta?'

Jan nodded.

'Well, I won't promise,' Esther said again, and smiled. 'Ah, there's the café.'

It was right on the quay and they could see their boat, gently rocking. There were bright umbrellas over the tables and as they sat down, Barry came along. He smiled.

'Good idea,' he said, and joined them.

CHAPTER FOUR

Jan enjoyed the talks she and Esther had on the balcony in the afternoons when Barry was away.

Jan found Esther's tales fascinating, for Esther's youth had been spent on a remote farm in Western Australia. It was so completely different from Jan's life in England that it amazed her.

'We were two hundred miles from our nearest neighbours,' Esther said, and laughed at Jan's horrified face. 'But we had lots of fun. We used to drive to our neighbours' for a game of tennis, a barbecue or a dance.'

'But what did you do all day?' Jan asked.

'Make clothes, cook, garden, look after the turkeys. There were four of us and we had our own tennis court and swimming pool, and when we were young, Mum taught us and we had lessons on radio. We were all such good friends, and then I met Barry...' Her voice softened as she said his name.

Jan looked at her, envious for a moment of Esther's uncomplicated love for Barry.

'Ludovic used to farm, he told me.'

'I know – or rather Barry knew him in those days. It must have been hard for Ludovic to give up the life he loved and come to a city like Sydney. Still, that's Ludovic. He'd always do what he considered right.'

'I can't understand Mrs Fairlie's behaviour...'

Esther laughed. 'She was probably due to come back and someone asked her to do a fresh lot of lectures. She loves doing them, the travelling, the V.I.P treatment, publicity, of it all. She has a secretary.' Esther's voice changed so much that Jan looked at her. Smiling ruefully, Esther went on: 'Was it so obvious? I can't bear Amanda Rowson, neither can Barry. She throws her weight around and acts like she's...' Esther laughed. 'Wait and you'll see what I mean. Mrs Fairlie owes a lot to her, though she'd never admit it, of course. And Amanda works for Mrs Fairlie because she has a plan.'

'A plan?' Jan looked enquiringly at her companion.

Nodding, Esther smiled.

'Amanda is beautiful, brainy and brutal. That's what Barry says. He's right, too. She'd be absolutely ruthless if the result was worthwhile, and in this case it is.'

Jan, with her feet tucked under her as she curled up in a cane couch, laughed. 'What's the result that's so wonderful?'

'Ludovic.'

Jan blinked with surprise. 'Ludovic? You mean they're...?'

'Oh no, nothing like that, but Amanda will get him, if any girl can. She acts like they were engaged when he's not around and both Barry and I dread the day they marry – if they do, of course – because we'll have to go. We couldn't take her.'

'Do you really think Ludovic loves her?' Jan said slowly, trying to imagine it, and then she remembered something Rab had said, that Ludovic, like all men, had an Achilles' heel and that one day a clever girl would hook him. Had Rab been thinking of Amanda Rowson? Jan wondered.

When Esther glanced at her watch, she jumped to her feet.

'That was lovely, Jan. Be seeing you. I'm working quietly on Barry. He sees you as different from most of Ludovic's friends, so maybe...' She smiled.

Jan smiled back. 'Good luck, Esther. I'm much happier here now I know you.'

Esther hesitated, one hand on the door.

'Jan, what made you come here in the first

place? I mean Ludovic has brought his friends here before, but never just one girl.'

'It wasn't Ludovic who asked me,' Jan said quickly. 'I had a letter from Mrs Fairlie inviting me to visit her.'

'Oh yes, I remember you telling me, now. I see,' Esther said thoughtfully, her face betraying the fact that she most certainly did not see. And then she slipped away.

Left alone, Jan thought about Ludovic and the brilliant and beautiful secretary, Amanda. An attractive name, Jan thought. Could Esther be right in what she believed – that Amanda wanted to marry Ludovic?

Hugging her knees, Jan thought about it. Would *she* like a man like Ludovic as a husband, a sarcastic man who could be patronising and yet change into someone kind and thoughtful? He was a man with whom you could never be secure, Jan told herself, shaking her head slowly so that her long black hair swung round, so men like Ludovic were certainly not for her. She preferred someone quiet and steady like Rab. Dear Rab!

How she enjoyed her mornings with him, and he enjoyed being with her, he often said.

'This is the life,' he had said one day with a quick smile, 'but doubly so with you by my side. It's much more fun when you have someone who shares your interests and can understand what you're talking about.'

Usually Rab didn't come at weekends, but the next Saturday when Ludovic, having arrived as usual on Friday, was planning what to do, Rab turned up, looking worried.

'I've got to get some photographs done to illustrate an article I've sold,' he told them. 'There's a deadline, so I hope you don't mind me turning up.'

Ludovic laughed. 'Of course not. Jan and I'll help you, won't we, Jan?' Jan nodded. She had been sitting quietly, almost afraid to speak, for Ludovic had come to the island the day before in one of his bad moods.

A little nervously she had asked him if anything was wrong.

'Everything's wrong,' he had snapped. 'My sister-in-law is in hospital in Melbourne, her secretary phoned me. Jarvis isn't well, either – had to go into hospital for treatment and is okay but rather weak.'

'Jarvis?' Jan had sat up anxiously. 'He'll be all right.'

She wondered if Felicity knew. Perhaps Felicity was back in Sydney. Jan had heard nothing from her sister, but that didn't surprise her, as Felicity was notoriously bad about writing letters.

'Yes, he'll be all right. Just messes up his studies.'

Ludovic had scowled, then produced a bulging briefcase and had gone to his study so that Jan had spent the evening alone.

Now as they sat on the verandah and Ludovic looked enquiringly at her, she nodded and smiled with relief, for everything would improve. A day's work with Rab would be something to interest Ludovic and distract his thoughts.

They went down to the lagoon the morning flew by. Sometimes Jan, listening to Ludovic laughing at some joke of Rab's, felt again the guilty discomfort she often felt because Ludovic had gone out of his way to help her enjoy this enforced holiday. Often she had felt inclined to tell him not to bother, but stopped herself, afraid of his sarcasm. It wouldn't be true to say she would be just as happy if he left her to herself, for having Ludovic come up each weekend always made the week go by faster.

Rab lunched with them and altogether it was a happy day for Jan. Late in the afternoon, Ludovic straightened from examining something in a small pool and looked at Jan.

'We're going dancing tonight, Jan,' he told her.

She was so surprised, she couldn't speak for a moment.

'We are?'

He nodded. 'We may be meeting some friends there. Anyhow I think it's time we introduced you to some of our night life. You'd better get back to the house, Jan, for you'll want to shower and have a short snooze.'

'Tonight?' said Jan. She was wearing pink jeans and a crumpled wet pale blue shirt. Her hair was dry and thick with salt.

'What better night than tonight?' Ludovic grinned. He stood, so tall and powerful with his hair ruffled from the breeze that had just sprung up. 'Do her good, don't you think, Rab?'

Rab looked startled at being drawn in, but nodded.

'Be a change for you, Jan. You work hard.'

She smiled at him. 'I enjoy it, Rab, it's great fun.'

'Good,' Ludovic butted in curtly. 'Get going, Jan, and doll yourself up. I'll help Rab. Did you get what you wanted?'

Ludovic turned to Rab, ignoring Jan, almost as if he was dismissing her.

'Yes, thanks to you and Jan. I'd never have got the photographs and specimens as well without your help.'

Jan walked back slowly. She hardly noticed the things that had first fascinated her, the flying foxes, or the pretty little birds, for she was too busy thinking.

What on earth, she asked herself, had made Ludovic suddenly decide to take her dancing? Could he have had a phone call that morning, for only the night before he had been in such a bad mood, and what had made him change so much? All day he had been in a good temper, joking, laughing, being his nicest self, and then, out of the blue, he announced that they were going dancing. How typical of Ludovic, she thought. He hadn't even *asked* her if she liked to dance. He had just said they were going to!

At the house, she showered and then looked through her wardrobe carefully. She had brought two formal dresses with her in case Mrs Fairlie proved to be the type of woman who insists on dressing for dinner. Now Jan studied them carefully.

Doll yourself, up, Ludovic had said, so she mustn't let him down.

One dress was a dark purplish-blue velvet dress, slim-making and long, lovely to wear, yet somehow she didn't feel it was quite what Ludovic had had in mind, so she turned to the other. It was made of Thai silk, a soft medley of different pastel shades of palest green, pink and yellow, all merging with two scarves fluttering from her shoulders.

She stroked the silk gently. What memories it aroused, she thought. Memories of the day she had bought it, spending far more money than she could afford because she wanted to impress George. She had worn it the first time George had taken her in his arms and nibbled lovingly at her ear, as he murmured what sounded like words of love and the abyss inside her had seemed to close. Today she could look at the dress without pain. She knew that it was this lovely island which had cured her of that childish infatuation, an infatuation born solely of loneliness.

Dressing carefully, she looked at her reflection in the mirror. She had to admit that she didn't look too bad! The understatement of the year, she told herself, laughing, for she really did look quite good. The wonderful colours did something to make her black hair, piled high, shine. Long pearl earrings and a matching necklace of pearls, presents from her mother before Jan left England, added to the sophisticated look Jan felt she had.

Just as she went into the hall, Ludovic came out of his room. He stood very still and then gave a long soft whistle.

'You look gorgeous,' he said.

She gave an elaborate curtsy, bowing her head.

'Thank you, my lord. You look pretty smooth yourself.'

For a moment he looked startled. Then he laughed.

'Of course. You haven't seen me dressed up before, have you?'

She shook her head. His dark silk evening suit showed off his strong body to perfection. His spotless white shirt had a ruffle down the front and he wore a red cummerbund round his waist.

'Just a moment...' he said, and vanished into one of the rooms, returning with a fur coat over his arm. 'You may need it coming back for sometimes a cold wind springs up,' he told her, taking her arm and leading her outside to the waiting carriage and horses.

The journey to the mainland was smooth. It was all so very romantic, Jan thought, as they sat in silence, although it could not be said that Ludovic was behaving romantically. Indeed, although he occasionally spoke to her, she had the feeling that he wasn't happy, that his mood was changing again. She wondered if she had unwittingly done something to displease him, yet that didn't make sense. It couldn't be that he thought she was overdressed? *He* had said 'doll yourself up' and she had obeyed.

Obeyed!

Her mind seemed to boggle at the word. Was she too getting into the way of doing immediately what Ludovic demanded? He had *told* her they were going to dance and he had *told* her to dress up, yet now he seemed strangely aloof.

This uncomfortable feeling of hers rather spoilt the journey through the beautiful water – they were getting glimpses of islands zooming up ahead, and then she saw the lights from the town they were making for, which came closer and closer until she could see the crowded busy roads, the illuminated advertisements as they flashed to and fro, and they came to the jetty.

A car with a chauffeur awaited them and, sitting by the now silent Ludovic's side, Jan glanced at him anxiously. If only she knew what had gone wrong, she might put it right, but it would be a miserable evening if Ludovic remained in this mood.

The hotel had a table reserved. The head waiter nearly fell over when he greeted them. Everywhere that Ludovic Fairlie went, he got V.I.P. treatment, Jan thought. In a way, it was fun to share it, but imagine living with this atmosphere all the time. No wonder Ludovic loved the quiet impersonal life he could enjoy on the island!

Jan began to talk, but gradually the words died away and her body grew tense, for Ludovic never answered and was staring ahead, frowning, his thoughts obviously miles away as they ate the delicious dinner. Afterwards they had coffee.

The orchestra was playing; several couples had taken to the floor when two people came to their table. Jan looked up, startled, and Ludovic leapt to his feet. A tall man with very short blond hair smiled at her and a girl, a really beautiful girl, Jan thought instantly, tall and making the most of her height by wearing a striking dress of black and white stripes, going diagonally, with a low neckline and her dark brown hair a mass of curls by his side.

'Ludovic!' she said, her voice husky as she held out both her hands to him.

'Amanda,' he said, and Jan caught her breath. So *this* was the brilliant and beautiful secretary who worked for Mrs Fairlie and planned to marry Ludovic, according to Esther, Jan thought.

Ludovic was smiling.

'Nice to see you, Amanda.'

She laughed, her eyes looking over Jan quickly and then seemingly dismissing her as if she was of no interest or value.

'Yes, I happened to bump into Peter and told him I was free for a few days and would like to fly up and see you, so he brought me.' She turned and looked at the silent man by her side. 'Dear Peter had his own plane, of course, so it was very simple.' She looked round her. 'I'm sorry we're so late. Ludovic, you've dined?'

'Yes.' Ludovic seemed to remember Jan, then, for he turned to her. 'Jan, I want you to meet Amanda Rowson, my sister-in-law's secretary. Amanda, this is Jan Shaw. Jan, this is Peter Frost ... Peter...'

Peter laughed and held out his hand.

'Glad to meet you,' he said. He had the usual suntanned skin, bleached hair and blue eyes that so many Australians had, Jan noticed.

She had taken an immediate dislike to Amanda, who had barely smiled at her then turned again to Ludovic, her hand on his arm, her eyes, with their incredibly thick black eye lashes, looking into his.

Ludovic moved slightly so that Amanda's arm dropped.

'Yes, we have dined,' he said. 'I suggest you eat now and Jan and I will dance. When you've finished, we'll all meet outside on the patio.'

Amanda opened her mouth as if to speak, then closed it as if she decided it was better to keep silent. Ludovic took Jan's arm in his hand and gently led her to the floor.

It was the first time she had danced with him. To start with she felt nervous, but he led her so smoothly that she relaxed and enjoyed every moment of it. Was there anything Ludovic could not do perfectly? she wondered. He did not speak, and his eyes were half-closed, the little frown showing between his brows which meant he was thinking. Jan recognised it, having seen it so often before. Was he pleased at Amanda's arrival? she wondered, and then thought that perhaps Amanda was the reason for this evening, because Amanda had apologised for being late. So, if Ludovic was in love with Amanda, he should be very happy now. Instead he was frowning. Perhaps she was the trouble, Jan thought, and wondered how she could say tactfully that she would be happy to wait in the boat until he was ready to go home. The thought made her smile.

Ludovic stared at her. 'What's the joke?' he asked.

She shrugged and looked into his eyes. She had often read that, close enough, you could see yourself reflected in your partner's eyes, but she had never believed it, or tested it. But tonight she could see herself, her eyes shining, her face so clear and pale, her dark hair gleaming.

His arm tightened round her.

'Yes, why?' he asked.

She was glad the music stopped them. They danced again and again, but Ludovic didn't repeat the question.

Later they joined the others on the patio, with long cool drinks before them. Ludovic and Peter went off for a few moments and Amanda and Jan sat in silence. It was such an embarrassing silence that Jan wondered how she could break it, and it came as a surprise when Amanda turned and looked at her.

'How much longer do you intend to stay?' she asked.

Jan stared back.

'Intend … to stay?' she repeated slowly. 'Mrs Fairlie invited me and I'm waiting to meet her,' she added, lifting her small chin. Amanda might be beautiful and brainy, but Jan was not going to be intimidated, she determined.

'You'll go, after you've seen her?' Amanda asked, her eyes hard with hate. 'You've made rather a fool of yourself, haven't you? Using Jarvis as an excuse to get involved with the wealthy Fairlies.' Her voice was maliciously sarcastic. 'But don't count your chickens before they're hatched. You haven't a hope. Ludovic is already bespoke.'

Jan managed an amused smile.

'So I understand.' She deliberately looked Amanda up and down. 'I'm not interested in Ludovic,' she went on. 'So you needn't be alarmed.'

Amanda's face went bright red and her hand came up – then stayed poised before lightly touching Jan's scarves.

'Beautiful material,' she said, just as the two men joined them.

The orchestra began to play and Peter Frost looked at Jan.

'Shall we?'

She stood up quickly, eager to leave Ludovic alone with his Amanda. Peter Frost took her hand as they walked to the dance floor. He smiled down.

'I'm green with envy,' he said.

She looked up at him. 'Why?'

'Because Ludovic always gets the pick of the bunch. I always said he could choose 'em.'

''Em?' she echoed.

'Birds, I mean. Birds like you and Amanda, with both beauty and wit. Of course it's easier for a man like Ludovic than a man like me.'

He danced well as he talked, but she didn't feel the same relaxation she had known in Ludovic's arms. She felt somehow that she didn't like Peter Frost. She wasn't sure why, but she distrusted him – which was absurd, for he was a friend of Ludovic's.

'Why is it easier for him?' Jan asked. The orchestra was playing one of her favourite tunes and she would have preferred to listen to it silently, but he seemed determined to talk.

'Because he's got the lolly, of course. Lovely gorgeous lolly that can buy you any girl you want.'

Jan's cheeks were hot. 'His lolly couldn't buy me!'

Peter chuckled. 'Want to bet? You're a Pommie?'

'I am.' She lifted her chin defiantly.

'I'm Australian.'

'I know.'

'How did you know?' he asked, laughing down at her.

'Because of your sun-tan and bleached hair and blue eyes,' she told him.

He laughed, delighted.

'You haven't asked me how I knew you were a Pommie.'

'I guessed it was my voice.'

'Partly; partly your attitude towards men. You're much more independent, not nearly so submissive as the Australian girls. They know we're the boss, but you've got to learn.' He laughed. 'Maybe I could be the one to teach you?'

Jan looked at him. 'I hate...' *Men,* she had been going to say, but stopped, for she realised it was no longer true. Barracuda Isle had taught her not to hate men!

'You hate me?' Peter chuckled. 'A lovely beginning, for from hate was love born.'

'You live in...?'

She deliberately changed the subject.

'Nowhere and everywhere. My parents travelled a lot and so did I. Still do.'

The music changed and when she turned to go back to the patio, Peter grabbed her hand.

163

'Don't go,' he laughed at her startled expression. 'Let's leave the lovebirds alone.'

Jan understood, then. When Peter and Ludovic had disappeared for a few moments, it had been to give Ludovic a chance to ask Peter to take Jan off his hands. For a moment she was filled with anger, then she realised she was being illogical. After all, if Ludovic loved Amanda...

'All right,' she said, and smiled at Peter Frost.

The music changed and the formal dance was over, so they jerked, swinging their limbs to the time of the music. As they laughed at one another Jan began to like Peter more and to drop her melodramatic feeling as regards his trustworthiness. However, after a while, she felt hot and exhausted, for they had had a hard day of work, fossicking with Rab, so she told Peter she would like to sit down.

'Sure.' He took her arm and led her from the floor, out into the garden. It was a different entrance, she noticed, and didn't lead to the patio. Here there was a long deserted terrace, smooth lawns leading down to seats, half hidden by well-cut bushes. 'It's cooler down here,' Peter explained, leading her down the steps, across the grass, to a seat by a cypress tree.

Jan drew a long deep breath. It was still hot out here in the garden. She sat down, sighing a little, for her feet hurt.

'You're happy on Barracuda Island?' Peter asked.

'Very.' She turned to smile at him. 'Have you been there? It's beautiful.'

There was a great round golden moon high up in the sky, myriads of twinkling stars, and there were coloured lamps hanging from the trees, just giving light enough to see vague shapes but not faces, she noticed as she looked round.

'I've never been there.' There was an odd note in Peter's voice. 'Ludovic only invites his girl-friends.' He laughed. 'We call it his harem. Only difference is that he only has one there at a time.'

Jan turned her head.

'Are you suggesting...' She could feel the adrenalin racing through her veins. 'Ludovic isn't like that.'

'I didn't mean you,' Peter said quickly. 'I know Mrs Fairlie invited you, didn't she? Or so they say.'

Jan sat stiffly. 'Who do you mean by we and they?'

'Ludovic's friends, of course.' Peter

sounded surprised.

'Fine friends they must be!' Jan's voice was cold. 'I received a letter from Mrs Fairlie, inviting me to stay.'

'I know. Amanda typed it. But it didn't say when, did it?'

'I don't understand. What do you mean...' Jan began, but Peter interrupted her.

'Why waste this lovely moment talking about Ludovic?' he said, and as he spoke he pulled her roughly towards him, so that she lay across his knees. As he bent and kissed her his hands wandered down her arms.

She acted without thought and following her immediate reaction. The sound as her hand slapped his face seemed to rebound in the quietness.

He released her so abruptly that she nearly slid to the ground, but she managed to regain her balance and scrambled, undignified but still furious, to her feet, then sat down.

'Well,' his voice was thick with fury, 'what a way to behave! Anyone would think you'd never been kissed before.'

'Of course I have, but just because I danced with you, it doesn't mean you can kiss me ... and certainly not like that!' Jan said angrily.

'Of all the freaks I've ever met!' Peter

nearly exploded. She could imagine his cheeks were bright red. 'Ludovic called you a Sleeping Princess waiting to be kissed by the right man and that then you'd come to life. I can't see anyone else risking a slap.'

'Jan ... Peter!' a voice called. It was Ludovic's. Thankful, Jan stood up just as Ludovic joined them.

'Sorry to break things up, but it's pretty late. I've said goodbye to Amanda, Peter. Thanks for giving her a lift. Nice meeting you.'

'Nice, indeed!' Peter almost snarled. Now she could see his face as he rubbed his cheek. 'Quite an experience! Goodnight!' He turned and hurriedly walked away.

Jan waited. How much had Ludovic seen? she wondered. But he said nothing, merely taking her arm.

'The car's waiting, Jan,' he said calmly.

As she walked, she realised she was trembling. Was it shock, she wondered, or disgust at the way Peter had handled her, grabbing and kissing – if kissing was the right word, she thought angrily. Those hands of his ... the cheek of it! Why, they'd only met that evening.

'Are you cold? Ludovic asked. 'You're trembling.'

'I am a bit,' she said, tempted to tell him what she thought of his friend. Then she decided not to, as obviously he had seen nothing.

In the car he put the fur coat on her, which helped a little, but on the boat she hardly spoke, only answering the few questions he put. The carriage was waiting for them, the horses so patient.

How romantic it would be if they were in love, Jan thought suddenly, the palm trees, tall and graceful, hardly stirring in the quiet stillness of the night.

Back at the house, she paused in the hall to say goodnight to Ludovic. But as she turned and began to speak, he caught hold of one of her arms and stopped her.

'Was it really necessary,' he began, his voice quiet but amused, 'to slap poor Peter's face? Surely not a very sophisticated reaction to a natural act on Peter's part. A pretty girl, dancing all evening with a handsome man, obviously enjoying his company, ignoring her host completely.'

Jan's cheeks burned.

'That doesn't give him the right to paw me, to slobber all over me like a mad creature. Why, I only met him tonight. I don't kiss every Tom, Dick or Harry I meet, you know. I'm pretty particular as to who I do kiss.'

The anger was rising inside her, almost too fast to control. She had no notion of how lovely she looked with her flashing eyes, angry-red cheeks and trembling mouth.

'Peter is a rich man,' Ludovic drawled the words, ignoring her anger. 'He would make a good husband, far better and richer than Jarvis.'

She tried to free herself from his grasp, but his fingers tightened, digging into her flesh.

'I'm not interested in money,' she shouted, 'I'm sick and tired of this eternal talk about money! It isn't important at all. It's about the least important of anything. When I marry, it'll be for love...' She swallowed, trying to control her anger but losing the battle, so she began again.

'How dare you!' she shouted. 'How dare you tell him I was waiting for the right man to kiss me? It was practically telling him to have a go!'

Ludovic laughed. Her hand flew, but he was too quick and caught hold of both her hands, holding them tightly.

'But I'm right, Jan,' he said. She knew he was laughing at her and she struggled help-lessly in his grasp. 'You *are* like a sleeping princess. You'll only come alive and be a warm human person after the right man has kissed you.'

Suddenly he pulled her towards him and put his arms round her. He held her so tightly that she could hardly breathe. Then he put one hand under her chin and gently tilted back her head, moving his face down towards her so that again that evening she could see herself reflected in his eyes. But she saw a different Jan, this time, a Jan with ruffled hair, red cheeks, and tears of fury in her eyes.

Then his mouth closed over hers...

She had no idea how long he kissed her. The touch of his warm hard lips, the warmth of his arm round her, seemed to wipe out her ability to think. The moment went on ... and on ... and on...

Then she realised something, something that both shocked and surprised her, for not only was he kissing her – but she was kissing him, her body trembling in his arms, her mouth eager as she responded to his.

He released her as abruptly as he had caught her to him and she staggered back, leaning against the wall, her arms spread out. She stared at him, unable to speak, trying to grasp the truth she had just learned.

'Well?' he said, and his voice was amused. 'That wasn't so bad, was it?'

He was laughing at her! For him, it was just a joke!

She was trembling a little, trying to come out of the confused state she found herself in. It couldn't be true! She bit her lower lip viciously, stood stiffly, now clasping her hands behind her back, digging her nails fiercely into the palms, trying everything she could think of to regain composure and keep him from discovering the humiliating truth.

Somehow she managed a light laugh.

'Ludovic, I never said I didn't *like* being kissed. It was just the way your friend did it. No warning, no ... well,' she managed a light laugh, 'no build-up.'

'Ah, I see you're a romantic. Peter is down to earth, a realist.'

'A realist?' Jan felt the anger growing inside her and was, for once, grateful for it. At least it would give her courage to carry on with this farce, to hide the truth. 'More like an animal, slobbering all over me. When a girl is kissed, she likes it to be done...'

'More professionally?' Ludovic made no attempt to hide his laughter. 'How did I show up?'

She looked up at him and managed another laugh. 'Not too bad,' she said lightly. 'Actually you're quite good,' she added, her voice flippant.

He laughed outright. 'Thanks. You'd give me a good reference, then?'

'I wouldn't know, honestly.' Her voice had changed, she realised with dismay. The flippancy had vanished and she was telling the truth. 'You see I haven't kissed many men and always it's been when I loved them. That does make a difference.'

She caught her breath with dismay, remembering the almost brotherly kisses of Frank, and the more sophisticated yet casual kisses of George. Ludovic's kisses had been completely different. So had her reaction to them. Never before had she found herself clinging to a man, her mouth responsive, her whole body trembling. She wondered whether he had noticed.

Ludovic moved away a little.

'I see.' His voice had changed, too. 'Yes,' he went on, his voice grave now. 'You're right, it does make a difference. Goodnight.'

Before she had time to answer him, he had gone, down the hall, to his room. There was silence after the door had clicked shut.

Somehow she managed to get to her

172

room. There she stood in the middle of it, hands pressed to her hot face.

It couldn't be true! It couldn't be. It mustn't ... but it was.

At last she crawled into bed, still shivering. Why, of all people, had she to fall in love with a man like Ludovic? Of all the stupid, irrational, humiliating, painful things to do! Jan buried her face in the pillow. She must get away, just as soon as she could ... and if Jarvis was landed in a mess, it wasn't her fault. This was something beyond her control.

She awoke to the sunshine and Lucy's hard-to-understand words as she brought the breakfast tray. There was a note on it.

'Have gone fishing with Rab. Guess you must be tired. We'll be back this afternoon. Rab is staying for dinner. Ludovic.'

Just as Ludovic dominated his world.

'Well,' she told herself, wondering why her voice, so quiet, was trembling, 'he's not going to dominate me. I'm getting out just as fast as I can. I'll tell him tonight.'

It was his writing – the first time she had seen it – huge sprawling letters that dominated the page.

She showered, then put on her bikini and went and swam in the enclosed lagoon behind the house. It was the only safe place to swim, for Ludovic had impressed on her the danger of swimming in the other lagoon, unless he or Rab were with her.

'There are some nasty fish around,' he had said, and added, 'Occasionally a shark comes in.'

Now as she floated on her back, looking up at the cloudless sky, and then at the palm trees on the white sand, she knew how much she was going to miss the island. She felt no desire to return to Lewes and her old life.

'You've got spoiled,' she told herself severely. 'It's time you went.'

Afterwards she lay on the sand, protected from the sun by a large orange sunshade. She lay still, eyes closed. She *must* go, of course she must go. What else could she do? Ludovic might find out and then how he would laugh. Just another scalp to hang on his belt, she reminded herself. One of so many. He probably would think she was after his money – as if she was interested in that! Money was useful, but it wasn't everything. Happiness came first.

The warmth of the air relaxed her, she fell asleep and dreamed. When she woke up, she was startled to find she could remember the dream. In her dream she had been walking down the aisle of a church to the sound of music. A bride, wearing a white lace frock with a long train, a veil hiding her face. The groom waited at the altar steps. He turned his head. There was a mask over his face. Both had stared at one another silently, unable to see the face of the other. And then she had turned and run, run down the aisle of the church. She had heard him racing after her, the sound of his shoes on the stone floor were so clear in the stunned silence of the congregation.

She had reached the door of the church and was out in the sunshine, and then he had caught her, holding her close, her whole body shivering as she felt her arms go round his neck. Then he lifted his hands and removed his mask. It was...

She must have awakened at that moment, for no matter how hard she tried, she could not remember the face.

Was it, she wondered, her subconscious self trying to marry Ludovic in her dream because she knew she would never marry him in reality?

Would never? she asked herself sarcastically, or *could* never? Somehow it was hard to imagine Ludovic asking her to be his wife!

And if he did…? She toyed with the crazy idea for a moment. Would she marry him if he proposed?

Of course she wouldn't, she thought angrily. Imagine life married to an arrogant, domineering, hateful…

A tiny lizard scuttled over the sand, began to climb her bare leg, changed his mind, did a quick turnabout and hurried away over the sand. Something had warned him that he was on alien soil, she thought, finding herself smiling at the thought. Well, wasn't that what she was on? Alien soil? Where she could only be hurt.

Why fool yourself, Jan Shaw? she asked herself sternly. You know very well that if Ludovic asked you to marry him, you'd faint for joy! At least be truthful!

She had showered and chosen her white sheath with the gold chain belt and was waiting for the men to come back from fishing when they arrived. Both looked tired and sun-flushed and she braced herself as Ludovic led the way on to the screened verandah.

'Had a good day, Jan?' he asked casually.

She had dreaded this moment and now it had come. Her tense body, braced for this moment of truth, slowly relaxed. Ludovic didn't know! He was just the same – friendly, impersonal. He probably looked on the scene the previous night as something that happened all the time. Probably he kissed every girl he met.

Inconsistently, and she realised this but it didn't help her at all, she was hurt by his casual attitude – yet she knew she would have been even more upset had he made it plain that he knew she loved him!

'Fabulous, thanks,' she said with a smile. 'Gorgeously lazy. I swam in this lagoon, then slept. I dreamt.'

She looked at him thoughtfully, a big, long-legged man stretched out on the wicker chair. He had just showered and his white shirt was immaculate, his white corded trousers neatly creased. He looked tired yet content, like a cat that has eaten the Sunday joint, Jan told herself viciously, momentarily hating him.

'Nightmare?' Rab asked. He too had showered and changed. His wet hair looked almost sandy for once. He yawned. 'By Jove, it was a fight!'

Ludovic linked his hands under his head.

'A good fight. Rab caught a thresher shark, Jan. Wish you'd been there to see it – a good battle. We'll make a good fisherman

of you yet, Rab, for all you're a Pommie!'
Ludovic added with a grin.

Lucy brought out a tray of drinks and ice.
It was very pleasant sitting there. Jan had to
admit to herself that she was going to miss
it all very much. Occasionally she gave
Ludovic a quick glance and was startled at
the effect it had on her. Her heart began to
pound. Of all the ridiculous crazy nonsense,
she scolded herself angrily, this was the
craziest. Maybe she had liked being kissed
by him, but that didn't mean... Didn't it? an
inner voice asked her. Didn't it show you
how much you love him? Face up to it, Jan
Shaw. You're madly in love with a man who
says you make him laugh.

The dinner was delicious, the oval walnut
table immaculately laid out, the crystal glass
sparkling, the silver shining.

'Esther is a good housekeeper,' Rab said as
he took a second helping of the delicious
cheese soufflé.

'And that's no lie,' Ludovic agreed.

It was over their coffee and liqueurs that
Jane made up her mind. She sat quietly
while the two men discussed their day,
going over the movements of the cunning
shark and their counter-movements, but Jan
was not listening.

She was preparing the speech she was going to make before she went to bed. In front of Rab, she was going to tell Ludovic that she was leaving.

She rehearsed the words silently: 'I've had a lovely holiday, but I must go. My mother needs me.'

That was a lie, of course, or was it? Maybe it was true? Maybe her mother did need her? The boutique was flourishing, but Mum was always having staff trouble. Perhaps she did need Jan? It was obvious that Felicity didn't, because she had leapt at the chance of dancing up north.

Jan tensed. Ludovic would look startled and then amused, she knew that. In his eyes would be the unspoken threat, unspoken only because Rab was there. But she knew what he would be saying silently to her.

'What about Jarvis?'

And what should she say? Tell him the truth? That it was all a mistake and she was not, and never had been, Jarvis's girl-friend? Or let him go on believing she was so that he would be glad to see her off on her way back to England – or rather falsely believing – his nephew would be safe when she was some ten thousand miles away!

The evening flew by and Rab began to say

he must be on his way. Jan knew her last chance had come. She drew a deep breath.

'Ludovic–' she began.

He turned at once. 'Yes?' Then he hit his hands together. 'Honestly, how stupid of me, Jan. I nearly forgot to tell you. Next weekend I'll be bringing Sara with me.'

Jan, her words dissolving because of his interruption, stared.

'Sara?'

Ludovic frowned. 'Sara, my niece, Jarvis's sister. Surely he's told you about her?' He sounded impatient. 'Jarvis! Honestly, that boy! Not an ounce of family feeling in him.'

Ludovic stood up and filled the glasses, then sat down again, letting his legs hang over the side of the chair.

'Well, Sara is being rather difficult. She's just sixteen and has been at a finishing school in Switzerland. I've heard from them and she's flying out. She's been asked to leave.'

'Expelled?' Jan was startled. Surely at an expensive finishing school, something really dreadful would have to happen before they expelled you? she thought.

'Well, as good as,' Ludovic confessed, rubbing his hand across his face. 'They wrote and said they felt they were not helping her as they thought they should. They felt it was the wrong… I think they used the word environment. They asked me to remove her.'

'But what for? Surely they said why?' Rab asked, leaning forward and obliterating for a moment from Jan's eyes the view of the beautiful crescent moon. 'Knowing Sara, I can't see her doing anything dreadful.'

'You don't know Sara,' said Ludovic. He shrugged. 'Those two kids – more trouble than they're worth! Anyhow, she's coming back and maybe you can talk some sense into her, Jan.'

'Me?' Jan's voice squeaked a little. She had been about to tell him she was leaving and now he was asking her to help him. 'I don't know what I can do.'

'You're her age group. Sixteen isn't far from nineteen, is it?' he asked.

A logical question, she told herself, yet it infuriated her. Was that how he classed her? With the teenagers? She didn't feel sixteen. She felt years older. She was no child.

Perhaps he read her thoughts, perhaps the flashing eyes and the red cheeks, always Jan's giveaway, might have told him how she felt, for he went on:

'You can remember what you felt like at sixteen, Jan. I can't. Something's upsetting

Sara and we can't find out what it is. I'd be grateful if you'd help me.'

She was even more startled. It did not seem possible that Ludovic could be asking *her* for a favour. And then she understood. Sara was going to upset the peacefulness of Ludovic's beloved island. She constituted a nuisance, and as such must be dealt with. Like all geniuses who are wise enough to relegate their duties, Ludovic was passing the buck to her! At least, that was how Frank would have put it, for he was always fond of long words and pedantic sentences.

'I … well, I haven't had much to do with sixteen-year-olds…' she began.

Rab leaned forward again.

'I think you could help her, Jan. I'll be here, too. Maybe we can sort out some of the poor kid's problems.'

Poor kid, Jan thought. She looked quickly at Ludovic and then at Rab. Was there more in this than she knew?

'I'll do my best,' she said, and stood up. 'I think I'll say goodnight. Have a good trip, Ludovic. See you next week,' she added as she left them.

She walked slowly to her bedroom. Well, that was that she was staying on. She wasn't leaving the island because maybe she could

182

help poor Sara.

In her room she let herself weep. It didn't help much, but even a little help was better than nothing. At least now she needn't leave the island and Ludovic. Face the truth, she told herself, you wouldn't have gone anyhow. I would if I had any sense, she replied, and her inner self laughed.

'Sense? If you'd any sense you'd never have fallen in love with a man like that. Be honest and face facts. You had no real intention of telling Ludovic you were leaving the island. You'd have found an excuse. You leapt at the chance to stay. Am I right?'

'As the Aussies said: "My very word, you're right",' Jan thought, and gazed in the mirror at her reflection.

'You're a fool,' she told herself. 'An absolute crazy fool.'

But there was no doubt in her mind now that she had accepted the truth. She was going to stay on the island. No matter how much Ludovic hurt her, how much she hated him, she wanted the chance to stay. She was only too painfully conscious of the reason.

CHAPTER FIVE

Next day when they were out on the coral reef, Jan asked Rab about Sara.

'Jarvis never mentioned her to me,' she said, puzzled, for although she and her sister Felicity shared very few interests they were fond of one another. Yet Jarvis, when he had visited them at Lewes, had never once mentioned Sara – or his mother, for that matter, Jan remembered.

Rab chuckled.

'At risk of having you knock my head off, Jan, I'd say that only one person exists in Jarvis's world, and that is Jarvis Fairlie.'

Jan sighed melodramatically.

'You're as bad as Ludovic! Always knocking poor Jarvis. Aren't we all selfish when we're young? We grow out of it.'

Rab put his head back and laughed.

'That's right, Granny. We do grow out of it as we grow older, but will Jarvis ever grow older?'

'Of course he will – one day.'

Rab bent to scoop up a small crab, turned

it over and examined it thoughtfully, the small magnifying glass to his eye.

'I reckon his uncle is treating him foolishly.'

'I couldn't agree more,' Jan said eagerly. 'I think Ludovic is positively beastly to him.'

Carefully, almost tenderly, Rab put the little crab down, watching it scuttle away to safety. Then Rab wiped his hands and looked at Jan.

'On the contrary, Jan, I think Ludovic is treating him much too softly. It's time Jarvis grew up. Let him fail his exams, if he's too darned stupid to work at them. He'll be sorry one day. Not that it really matters, because he can still get a job. I'd say to Jarvis if he was my nephew: "This is your last chance. Pass your Finals and work in the firm or I cut your allowance down to nothing. You're old enough to earn your own living and it'll do you the world of good"!'

Jan was shocked. 'But Jarvis has a lot of money coming to him.'

'Precisely. He's being mollycoddled now and will then be rich. What he needs is a bit of reality, to discover that it costs money to have your suit cleaned twice a week, that drinks are expensive, huge sports cars even more so. That it costs money to buy petrol to run a car, to call long-distance to Paris, and all the things Jarvis does automatically and without any idea of what these things cost.'

Jan stared at him. 'Aren't you being harsh? It sounds unlike you, Rab.'

Rab grinned. 'I grew up the hard way. Maybe I'm just jealous. I could do with some of Jarvis's money. Seriously, though, Jan, I think Jarvis needs responsibility, to be treated as an adult and not as a delinquent child to be humoured one moment and then punished the next. The poor lad's had a difficult time. When his dad was alive, it wasn't much better and now his mother lets him do just as he likes, and then Ludovic lectures him. Jarvis doesn't know where he is or where he's making for.'

'You could be right...' Jan said thoughtfully. It was a view she had never thought of. If Jarvis always had all the money he needed, how could he ever appreciate it or know how to handle it? 'But tell me about Sara?'

'There's not much to tell. I only see her here at holiday times. She comes and helps me, just as you do. She has a pretty miserable time.'

Later, as they packed Rab's things, Jan tried again.

'Why are you sorry for Sara?'

Rab scratched his head.

'You'll know when you see her – a nice kid having a lousy life. No wonder she's a problem child.'

'Perhaps all sixteen-year-olds are hard to understand,' Jan conceded. 'I remember my sister was. Mum nearly went out of her mind. Nothing she could do was right.'

'I think in this case, it goes deeper. See you tomorrow, Jan,' said Rab, striding off to his waiting boat, waving his hand.

Jan walked slowly through the trees. A burst of song broke the quietness as a cluster of small green parakeets swept up into the air. But she didn't notice them, because she was thinking.

After lunch, Jan, having showered beforehand and changed into blue shorts and a bikini top, went to lie under the umbrella on the silvery-sanded beach. She heard the sound of voices, but was half asleep and when a shadow fell over her and an angry voice spoke, Jan sat up abruptly.

A girl was standing there, a tall, thin girl with long blonde hair and hard, angry eyes.

'What do you think you're doing here?' she demanded. 'This is private property. You're trespassing.'

Half asleep, Jan struggled to her feet.

'I most certainly am not,' she said indignantly. 'I'm a guest here.'

'A guest?' the girl laughed. 'Whose?' She was wearing an expensive-looking green suit.

'Mrs Fairlie's. Who are you?' Jan asked.

'Mrs Fairlie's? A likely story! You're not Ludovic's guest, by any chance, are you?' The girl's voice changed, became wary.

'I am not. I'm Mrs Fairlie's. Look,' Jan was beginning to get annoyed, 'just who are you? I might think you were the trespasser.'

'I'm Ailsa Connaught...' The girl paused dramatically as if certain that that would ring a bell and Jan look suitably impressed. But Jan didn't.

'I'm no wiser. Are you a friend of Ludovic's?'

'A friend?' Ailsa Connaught gave an odd laugh. 'I suppose you might call it that, though sometimes I wonder why I ever speak to him,' she said bitterly. 'So Mrs Fairlie invited you here – how very convenient for Ludovic. I suppose he flies up at weekends.'

'Yes, he does, but...'

Ailsa laughed. She looked beautiful.

'He used to bring me here at weekends ... it was great fun. Always plenty of guests.

188

Well, he stopped and I heard nothing more. I've been away in Brazil and only just got back, so thought I'd look in and see if he was here. He used to leave on Tuesdays.'

'Now he leaves on Mondays.'

'Oh!'

The two girls stared at one another warily, each waiting for the other to attack.

Jan stiffened. She had a feeling this girl could be malicious. Was she one of Ludovic's heartbroken girl-friends? Not that Jan could blame Ludovic if he had thought himself in love with Ailsa, for she was very lovely and probably moved in his class of friends.

'Are you in love with Ludovic?' Ailsa asked abruptly.

The question took Jan unawares. She caught her breath. This girl mustn't know the truth, whatever happened.

'Jarvis is my favourite,' she said quickly. Of course it was a lie. Every bone in her body ached for sight of Ludovic. Where was he now? she wondered. Still in the air, flying high above the clouds? Or was he already in his office, his beloved island forgotten? 'Jarvis wants to marry me,' Jan added, thinking that if Ailsa saw Ludovic she might tell him that and it would not only protect

189

Jarvis, but hide the truth from Ludovic.

'Marry you?' Ailsa put back her head and laughed. 'Jarvis marry a Pommie? Not on your life! Besides, that's all arranged. His mother's got it all worked out. Jarvis will marry Lucille Lucknow, one of the wealthiest girls in the country. She's still at school, of course, so Jarvis is being given a chance to sow his wild oats and get that part of his life done before he settles down. Marry you! The Fairlies have more sense than that. You must be naïve,' she added scornfully. 'The Fairlies don't marry for love. They never have done. They marry to increase their riches, to improve the family income. Not for love,' she said sneeringly.

Jan was thinking fast. Things began to add up. She had been brought here out of Jarvis's way, not to let him go on with his student work, but to give him a chance to get tired of her and find someone else. It didn't matter, really, with whom Jarvis was involved so long as marriage didn't enter into it.

Ailsa Connaught had turned away, but now she looked back.

'So long as you've not lost your heart to Ludovic, I'm not interested, but remember one thing – if anyone's going to get him, it's me. I've known Ludovic for years. He doesn't know how I feel or he'd run a mile so fast I wouldn't know where he'd gone.' She laughed. 'There are better ways to work it than chasing him. One day I'll hook him, make no mistake,' she added savagely, and walked off.

Jan sank to the hot sands, hugging her knees, staring blindly at the sea. Ailsa was beautiful, but so was Amanda. Both were determined, Jan told herself, and wondered if it was Ailsa that Rab had meant when he said that, one day, a clever beautiful girl would discover Ludovic's Achilles' heel and handle him? Or was it Amanda?

Shivering a little despite the heat, Jan went to swim. Not that it helped, she found, not even floating on her back, gazing up at the pale blue sky as she shut her eyes, but she could only wonder if it was Ailsa walking down the church aisle ... or Amanda? Either were hateful thoughts, she decided, so turned over in the warm water and swam ashore. She wondered what sort of wife either would make Ludovic, but again came another question as Jan wondered what sort of husband Ludovic would make.

Ashore the heat dried her instantly, but Jan realised that she wouldn't mind *what* sort of husband Ludovic might be if only he would marry her.

The days of the week flew by and then came Friday. Ludovic was bringing Sara and Jan looked forward to meeting her. It would be fun to have a companion to talk to … that is, of course, if Sara was willing to be friendly. Sixteen-year-olds could be difficult at times. Jan remembered how Felicity had behaved only the year before.

Friday came, but no Ludovic or Sara. Jan began to worry. Could something have happened? she thought anxiously. A plane crash? She decided to write to her mother and went to her room, then returned restlessly to the hall. Should she ask Esther if Barry *had* gone in to meet them, but if he hadn't he would surely have told her, Jan thought. She saw the drawing room door was ajar and Ludovic was there. He heard her heels on the polished floor and turned.

'Hi. I wondered where you were,' he said, and she noticed it was his casual friendly voice. 'I got held up – a strike. Afraid poor Sara's in a worse state, having to spend the night in Sydney. Her plane was very late.'

Couldn't you have waited for her? Jan wanted to ask, but decided it was none of her business.

As if able to read her mind, Ludovic smiled.

'I arranged for Jarvis to meet her and take her out to dinner. They get on better together when I'm out of the way. Maybe Jarvis'll be able to knock some sense into her.'

He gave her a cold drink and they went to sit on the screened verandah.

'What sort of week?' Ludovic asked casually.

'Very pleasant.'

Jan looked at her hands, twisting her fingers together. She was afraid to look at him in case he saw the truth. Surely it must be showing in her eyes? She loved this man and hated him, too, at times. A strange mixture. But she knew one thing – when he was there, everything changed and came alive, was brighter, more lovely. Even the palm trees seemed to straighten, the birds to sing more. Then she remembered and looked up.

'By the way, you had a visitor on Monday. She hoped to catch you here. She's back from Brazil.'

'Brazil?' Ludovic frowned. 'Brazil?'

'Yes, Ailsa Connaught.'

'Oh, Ailsa! She's always chasing me. Thinks I don't know it.' He laughed. 'I'm not a fool. Girls have always chased me, so I recognise all the symptoms.'

'I don't chase you.'

Jan felt the familiar anger stirring in her. Why must he throw his weight around and be so arrogant?

He looked at her, his eyes amused.

'So far, you haven't,' he admitted. 'But I expect it any moment. You seem to be weeding out the wealthy men, you know. First, your neighbour, Frank Sutcliffe, in England, but he wasn't much good, was he? Not after you'd met Jarvis and realised what wealth there was out here. Then there was George Sugden, but you soon threw him out. Then Jarvis ... and now? Me? I thought you'd fall for Peter. He's much wealthier than Jarvis, you know.'

Jan stared at him. She felt frozen.

'How do you know all that about me?'

He laughed. 'I have spies. You'd be surprised what I know about you. It's all in the file in my office.'

She stood up, trembling with anger.

'I've never been so insulted in my life! I think you're ... you're impossible!' The words poured out of her mouth. 'Hateful, conceited, arrogant, beastly...' she spluttered, and stopped speaking, for he was shaking with laughter. 'Why you...'

He caught her arm as she went to smack his face.

'Please, Jan, I'm sorry. I'm only teasing you. Where's your sense of humour? I only did it to make you mad. I've got no file, though I do know all about you.' He was still laughing.

She was shaking and sat down near him, for he still held her arm.

'Why?'

She couldn't believe it. He had said he was sorry. He had actually apologised!

'Why? Because you look so much prettier when you get mad, Jan. It's the truth.' He stopped laughing. 'I'm sorry,' he repeated. 'I didn't mean to upset you.'

'A joke!' She swallowed and saw him through a mist of tears she wouldn't shed. 'You have a strange sense of humour.'

'I know, but you can't change a tiger's stripes.'

'I thought it was spots!'

'No, that's a leopard,' he said with a smile. 'Another drink?' he asked, his voice casual.

It wasn't until hours later, when Jan was lying awake in bed, that she realised she had been so surprised by Ludovic's apology that she had completely overlooked the real reason for her anger.

Ludovic had made it appear that she was insulted and furious because he had spied on her. Well, in a way, that was true, but it wasn't the real reason. What *had* upset her was the suggestion that she was looking for the wealthiest husband and had discarded Frank and George, and perhaps Jarvis, in an effort to find the richest man she could! As if money mattered all that much. Though it did seem to matter to Ludovic, she knew.

Tossing and turning in the hot room, Jan tried to sleep, but her thoughts spun round and round in circles and always she came back to the same thought.

Why was it so important for Jarvis to make a marriage of convenience? *Why* must he marry a very rich girl? Wasn't he one of the wealthiest young men in Australia? Or wouldn't he be when he was twenty-five years old? Then why did he need to marry money? she wondered. Yet it must be urgent and important in Ludovic's eyes as otherwise he surely wouldn't go to so much trouble to keep her out of the way, Jan thought, even producing a horrible creature like Peter to distract her attention. Then she felt ashamed. Peter was all right. Maybe she had acted hastily, but if he had gone about it more ... well, with more ... what was the word? Romantic way, Ludovic would have said sarcastically. Yet what girl liked to be grabbed and kissed without any build-up? Kisses didn't mean a great deal, but ... well, no girl wanted to kiss just anyone, did she? she asked herself. All the same, maybe she should have handled the situation more sophisticatedly. She tried to imagine how Ailsa or Amanda would have behaved at such a time. Her thoughts went back again to the money. If Ludovic insisted that Jarvis marry for money why didn't Ludovic do the same? Perhaps that was what he was planning and still looking for – the richest girl?

Finally she fell asleep, and dreamt, only to awaken next morning with the frustrated feeling that if only she could remember what she *had* dreamt about, it might answer her question.

She had no chance to talk to Ludovic alone that day, for Rab joined them and they went fishing. Jan enjoyed this fishing expedition better, for she had a sympathetic companion and while Ludovic and Barry battled with a huge fish, Jan and Rab could talk. That evening he stayed to dinner and the two men got absorbed in a discussion about a certain kind of fish, believed prehistoric, that had been found. Jan began to yawn. The long day in the sunshine had tired her, so she decided to go to bed – reluctantly, though, wishing she had a chance to talk alone with Ludovic.

At the door she paused, turning her head to stare at the two men, their heads bent now over a map as they worked out currents in the ocean, and where the strange fish could have come from. Jan let her gaze linger on Ludovic's fair bleached hair, his strong face, firm chin. Was he really the hateful arrogant man she thought him? If so, why did she love him so much?

Ludovic looked up and stared at her. She swallowed nervously. Had her eyes given away their secret? she wondered. Then Ludovic smiled.

'Sleep well,' he said. 'Pleasant dreams.'

'Thanks,' she mumbled, and hurriedly closed the door, leaning against it. She had never known love would be like this. The yearning to be with him, to have him to herself, to hear his voice, see his smile. Just to know he was there. In the morning, when she awoke, he would be gone and she wouldn't see him until Friday at the earliest. Pleasant dreams, he'd said. Well, she dreamed most nights and she was sure they were about him, but she could never remember them and only had these frustrating, teasing half-memories.

It was three days later that Sara arrived. Barry had come to the house just after Jan had dressed. He had smiled, his usual formal smile.

'Thought you'd like to know, Miss Fairlie's coming today. I'm going over to meet her. Like to come?'

'Thanks, Barry, I'd love to go. I'll just run down and tell Rab.'

'No hurry, the plane doesn't arrive until mid-afternoon,' Barry told her. 'Be at the jetty about two o'clock. Okay?'

'Fine,' said Jan.

Suddenly she felt excited, for she had realised something. Sara had been having dinner with Jarvis. Jarvis would certainly feel able to give his sister a note for Jan! Ludovic had said the brother and sister got on well, so Jarvis was sure to confide in Sara and tell her how Jan was helping him. Then he would give Sara a letter for Jan and she would know if she was really helping him and Felicity by staying up here.

The journey was pleasant. For once, Barry was friendly, much more like the man she knew on their fishing expeditions. He talked to her of fishing trips they'd made and Ludovic's dream and his.

'One day we're going to sail round the world. People have done it, but we're planning a different way. The hardest way,' he grinned. 'It'll be beaut. Trouble is he's so busy.'

'What about your wife? Won't she be worried if you go?' Jan asked.

'Esther?' Barry chuckled. 'She'll accept anything if it makes me happy.'

Jan knew he was right. She would be the same if Ludovic was her husband.

The airport was crowded, with tourists pouring in by the hundreds. Jan stood by Barry's side, waiting, and when she saw the tall slender girl with short curly red hair and very plain green suit, she tried to see a resemblance to Jarvis. There was none whatever.

'Barry!' the girl said with a quick, almost eager smile. 'It's good to be back.'

Then she saw Jan and her face changed, became wary, her eyes changed too. It was as almost as if she was tense.

'Miss Jan Shaw.' Barry introduced formally, and collected Sara's luggage, leading the way to the car.

Sara looked at Jan and frowned.

'Ought I to know who you are?'

Jan smiled back. 'Didn't Jarvis tell you about me?' Some of her excitement was fading and it vanished when Sara shook her head. 'Ludovic told me you were dining with Jarvis, and I was sure he'd tell you.'

'I didn't have dinner with Jarvis. I wasn't well. He phoned me, but we don't talk the same language.' Sara's face had a strange habit of changing. One moment she looked vulnerably young, and then suddenly she looked almost hard and sophisticated. 'I've no patience with him,' she went on. 'He's so weak he never fights Uncle.'

'Uncle...' Jan began, and stopped. Of course, Sara meant Ludovic. 'I rather hoped Jarvis would send a message,' she said. 'You see, I'm only here because of him.'

'Jarvis?' Sara turned to look at Jan, puzzled. 'Jarvis asked you here?'

They were at the car, Barry bustling around before sliding behind the driver's seat and starting the engine.

'It's a long story,' Jan said. 'You must be tired. I know I was, after flying up here.'

Sara nodded. 'I am, a bit. I wasn't well in Sydney either. But I'll be all right on the island. I always am.'

'You like the island?' Jan asked.

'And how!' Sara gave a low, almost bitter laugh. 'It has only one thing wrong with it and that's the fact that it belongs to my uncle. I hate loving anything that belongs to him.'

'Actually I was invited here by your mother,' Jan told her.

Sara's face changed again. She looked amazed.

'My mother asked you?'

'Yes, well, I might as well tell you the lot,' said Jan. 'Your mother was worried about me. She thought Jarvis wanted to marry me and...'

'Did he?'

'I'm sure he didn't, but your mother thought he did. We were just friends. She asked me to stay and ... well, give Jarvis a chance to take his Final exams without me there to distract him,' Jan laughed. 'So here I am waiting to meet your mother.'

'How long have you been on the island?' Sara asked.

Jan told her, amazed at how fast time had flown.

'Mother'll turn up some time,' Sara said. 'You never know where you are with her. She's so terribly busy.'

'I'm sure she will,' Jan said cheerfully. 'She'll want to see you.'

Sara turned her head swiftly, her cheeks suddenly red, but at that moment, the car stopped near the quay and Barry, getting out, broke up the conversation.

On the boat, Sara and Barry talked and Jan sat quietly watching the girl. It was amazing how quickly Sara changed. She was like her uncle in that respect. With Barry she was relaxed, more of a happy schoolgirl on holiday – then, if she looked up and saw Jan sitting there, she seemed to retreat as if afraid of what questions might be asked.

Jan looked at the islands they passed, the cruisers speeding along, the glorious emerald-green of her beloved palm trees, bent for ever against the cruel winds.

Jan saw the look on Sara's face as the island came into view.

'It's lovely,' said Jan, trying to be friendly. 'I don't think I've ever seen any place so beautiful.'

'You weren't bored here, or lonely?' Sara asked as they went ashore.

'Oh no. I go fossicking with Rab. He says you help him, too.'

'Rab's all right. I like him,' said Sara. 'He's different from Uncle.'

Sara and Jan got into the carriage and the black horses trotted demurely along the earth road. Sara laughed.

'Isn't it gloriously Victorian being driven like this!'

'Yes,' Jan laughed. 'Out of this world.'

'Look, *did* my mother write and invite you to the island?' Sara asked unexpectedly.

'Yes. Your uncle came to my flat in Sydney with the invitation,' Jan chuckled. 'Honestly, I must have looked a sight! I'd just had a shower and had put on my towelling coat, washed my hair and there was a ring at the bell. I went and there was … was your uncle. I hadn't a clue as to who he was and then he said: "I'm Jarvis's uncle" and of course I knew. Jarvis had often talked about his uncle.'

'He hates him as much as I do,' Sara said calmly, 'but he's scared of him. I'm not. I do everything Uncle dislikes. That's why I got expelled – to make him mad.' She laughed. 'I'm not easily beaten.'

'Why were you expelled?' Jan asked, a little nervously.

'I had a boy-friend. We used to meet at nights in the garden. We wrote to one another, and they found one of his letters.'

'But you said *you* made them expel you?'

204

Sara laughed.

''Course I did. There wasn't a boy-friend. I wrote the letter and made up the whole story. They're very strict and I really shocked 'em.' Sara laughed again. 'I've got a good imagination, you know.'

The carriage stopped and Sara jumped up, leaving Jan behind as she ran into the house. As Jan went into the hall, Sara came out of one of the always closed doors.

'Just making sure Lucy's cooking my favourite dinner,' Sara said cheerfully. 'Know something, Jan? I've been thinking about it. Knowing my uncle I bet he got you up here by tricking you. He knew you wouldn't come unless you had a proper invitation from my mother. He's cool, all right. I bet you Mum doesn't even know you exist.'

Jan stared at her, startled for a moment, and then remembering that she, too, had thought exactly the same thing.

'No – she did, because her secretary knew.'

'Oh, *that* woman,' Sara sniffed as if she, like the Ryders, disliked Amanda.

'I did wonder, though, Sara,' Jan went on, 'because he's capable of anything. He got me here by lie ... and has kept me by moral blackmail.'

She stopped abruptly as she saw the excited pleasure on Sara's face.

'Moral blackmail? Oh, boy!'

Jan wished she hadn't spoken so frankly.

'Hadn't you better have a shower ... you must be tired,' she said.

Sara winked wickedly.

'I know. Walls have ears and our beloved uncle has spies. Right, Jan, we'll talk later. See you!' Sara finished, her voice friendly, as she went into her bedroom.

Jan did the same. She had a shower, changed into a clean yellow frock and went to stand on her verandah. On every side were the palm trees. They should have delighted her, but for once they didn't. Nor did the gorgeous colour of the water, or the sunshine ... for she felt ashamed, as if she was guilty of something. She knew what it was. She wished she hadn't said such things of Ludovic. It only added to Sara's resentment and hatred and...

After all, let's face it, she told herself severely, for all she knew, Ludovic might really be worried about Jarvis's future and have acted for his good.

And then she was angry with herself. Why should she make excuses for the 'Master of Barracuda Isle'? How he must love the sound of those words; they gave him power, the power he loved. Power to rule others, to determine their lives, to rule them.

Ludovic *could* have treated the whole affair differently. He could have got in touch with her, perhaps even asked her out to lunch and put the whole problem before her. Discussed in a civilised way, they could have arranged something. Jan might have got a job in Melbourne or Adelaide. There had been no reason to trick her into coming up here – or was it because he couldn't trust her to stay away from Jarvis? Because he didn't trust anyone? And she had always believed that those people who couldn't trust others were the people who were not to be trusted themselves!

She was sitting on the screened verandah when Sara joined her. She was wearing green jeans that matched her eyes, and a yellow blouse and sandals. Her red hair was slightly ruffled, her eyes bright with curiosity, as she curled up in one of the wicker chairs.

'Jan,' Sara began eagerly as if she couldn't wait to talk, 'I thought you were on Uncle's side, one of his spies, you know. That's why I wasn't very friendly. I thought he'd got you here to look after me and try to make me mend my ways.'

Jan laughed. 'Think I'd have succeeded?'

Sara stretched her slender body luxuriously. 'Of course not. I'm tough. Just like...' She stopped, her face momentarily disturbed.

Jan smiled sympathetically. 'Just like your uncle. You are, you know. Not to look at, of course, but you have the same abrupt changes of mood, the same determination.'

'I wish it hadn't to be him I'm like...' Sara said slowly.

'He has some good qualities, you know,' Jan suggested, 'as well as bad ones.'

'I suppose we all have. It's just that ... that ever since Dad died, Uncle has taken over and bullied us around. Especially Jarvis ... and ... and...'

The door swung open and Lucy was there, a big beam on her face, as she carried a tray of glasses, ice and lemonade.

'Lovely, Lucy.' Sara bounced to her feet like a child. 'Just what we needed, eh, Jan?'

She waited until Lucy had left them, then turned to Jan.

'Now how has Uncle been practising moral blackmail on you?' she demanded.

Jan laughed. 'I think I exaggerated.'

'I'm sure you didn't. Tell me, Jan.'

Jan hesitated. Then she decided that if Sara was to be her friend, they must be honest with one another. She felt safe with Sara who so obviously hated her uncle that she would never tell him what Jan told her.

'It's a long story, Sara, but I'll be as brief as I can.'

Sara stretched herself out happily in her chair.

'Take as long as you like. I can't wait to hear!'

Jan began at the beginning, describing briefly their house just outside Lewes, in Sussex, and the boy next door, Frank, whom she had always known and how they had somehow drifted into an engagement.

'Then one day I realised Frank was a stranger. I had dreamed up a man and pretended Frank was him. Frank was a dear but oh, so stodgy. Then we met Jarvis. He was over on a course. He and my sister Felicity fell in love.'

'Felicity. Pretty name,' Sara said. 'Is she older than you?'

'No, younger. She's seventeen and I'm nineteen.'

'And I'm sixteen,' Sara chimed in. 'Do go on.'

So Jan did, describing Felicity's heartache

when Jarvis returned to Australia, Felicity's chance of a job out here, their mother's wish that Jan went with Felicity.

'We took a flat in Kings Cross, you know it?' Jan said, and Sara nodded. 'Then Felicity got this wonderful chance of a tour up north. She'd have been mad to refuse it, so off she went. And I fell in love with George.'

Sara wriggled excitedly.

'How smashing. Was he super?'

'Yes, in a way. Smooth, sophisticated. I guess I was just lonely, but I fell for him, and then he ditched me...'

Sara stopped smiling, her eyes grew wide.

'Ditched you?'

'Yes, it was my own fault, of course.' Jan was twisting the tassels on the cushion on her chair. 'It was fun being with him, but I think he thought I was getting possessive and thinking it might end in marriage, so he told me frankly that he would marry for money.'

'And you haven't any?' Sara said sympathetically.

'Only what I earn. Mum has a boutique in Lewes, but she isn't wealthy. Not like Ludo ... like your uncle.'

'Uncle!' Sara sounded disgusted. 'He's

stinkingly rich.' Her face brightened. 'But so will Jarvis be one day. He inherits a lot from Granddad.' She paused. 'You're not in love with Jarvis, are you?' she added worriedly. 'I still don't see how Uncle Ludovic black-mailed you.'

Jan sighed. 'It's all so involved. Anyhow, to go back, George dropped me like a hot potato and I was ... well, upset.'

'Understatement of the year!' murmured Sara.

Jan laughed. 'You're right. Oh, being jilted is awful, Sara, because you seem to be drifting in space. Nothing matters, yourself least of all. No one loves you, wants you. You're just utterly alone. Then Jarvis came to see Felicity and found me crying. He was marvellous. They took me out; so did he after Felicity went north and he taught me to laugh again. Honestly, Sara, he was ... well, wonderful.'

Sara shook her head thoughtfully.

'That's a new Jarvis to me. You're sure he isn't in love with you?'

'Quite, quite sure. He never stopped talking about Felicity. Well, I decided I couldn't work in the same firm as George, so I gave up my job, and then one day just as I was washing my hair, your uncle walked in and

told me he and your mother were concerned about my friendship with Jarvis, and
that Jarvis wanted to marry me. I was
surprised. In fact, I just didn't believe it.
Then I thought maybe Jarvis was using me
as a screen.'

'A screen?'

'M'm. You see, so as to hide Felicity. You
know how your uncle is, stuffy and pompous...' Jan stopped, seeing the delight in
Sara's eyes, and once again felt guilty because
Ludovic wasn't there to defend himself.
'Well, anyhow, I thought they might disapprove even more of Felicity, who dances,
and I guessed Jarvis had used me to ... well,
to distract their attention. I thought he was
pretending to be in love with me so that...'

'Uncle would get to work on you,' Sara
said triumphantly. 'How clever of you to
work it out. So you pretended it was true.'
She chuckled happily. 'Poor old Uncle! I bet
he'd be mad if he knew.'

Jan laughed. 'I bet he would. But that's
what I mean by moral blackmail. He said
Jarvis's mother wanted to meet me so that
we could get to know one another. Then
when I got here and found ... well, your
mother wasn't here and I got a bit worried
and said I wanted to go back to Sydney, he

212

laughed. He told me I wasn't a prisoner, that I could go back tomorrow but that Jarvis might not be pleased.'

Sara leaned forward, her face excited.

'What did he threaten to do to Jarvis?'

Again Jan hesitated. Was she making a melodrama of this? Had she the right to tell Sara and add to her hatred of her uncle?

'He said he'd halve Jarvis's allowance and ask for his own car back. He told me he'd lent Jarvis a car and I knew how Jarvis'd hate this, and after all, Jarvis had helped me...'

'So?'

Jan shrugged.

'I stayed here. What else could I do? I wrote to Jarvis and managed to go ashore and post it without them seeing the letter, but I've had no answer from Jarvis at all. That's why I hoped he'd talk to you. You see, if Jarvis wouldn't *mind* what his uncle did to him, I could leave, couldn't I?'

Sara ran her hand through her red hair.

'Want to leave?'

'I can't stay here for ever.'

A bell tinkled and Sara jumped up.

'Time to eat. Tomorrow Rab'll be here?'

'Of course. He comes every day.'

'Good oh! He's a friend of mine,' Sara

said, leading the way, almost dancing.

Jan walked more slowly following her, feeling guilty because of their talk. How, she wondered, did you manage to both hate and love a man at the same time?

CHAPTER SIX

Now that Sara was on the island, Jan found it even more pleasant than before. It was fun to go fossicking with Rab, for Sara worked hard and got so excited when she found something of interest. In the afternoon the two girls usually swam in the enclosed lagoon and then lay in the hot shade, talking. But though they were good friends, Jan found there was one real obstacle between them – Sara's mother. Jan longed to know more about the strange woman who had invited her and then forgot all about it – but Sara never mentioned her.

Oddly, enough, Sara was quite willing to talk about Jarvis, her Uncle Ludovic, and about her father whom she obviously adored.

Then the rain came.

It was without warning except that suddenly there was a howling sound and the palm trees were misted by rain, their fronds dancing wildly in the wind and rain. The trees looked crazy, bent nearly double against the wind and the sky thick with dark grey low clouds.

'Oh no!' Sara exclaimed in dismay. 'Rab won't come.'

'Maybe he will this afternoon, if it doesn't last.'

But it did last, and the two girls played records and talked, for Sara loved to hear about Jan's life in England and the boutique her mother ran so successfully.

'She words so hard,' Jan said, 'she needs a holiday. I wish she could come out here, because she'd love it. Does your mother like the island?' Jan asked unthinkingly, and then regretted it, for she knew how Sara hated any mention of her mother, but perhaps the long hours they had spent together had reassured Sara for this time she didn't retreat but answered the question.

'She hates it, but then she hates anything to do with Uncle Ludovic.'

'But why?'

Sara shrugged. 'Well, Jan, it's hard to explain. You'd have to have known Dad really. He was so different from Uncle Ludovic. Dad was a dreamer, a happy man, and we had such a lot of fun. He loved us and ... and I know that Uncle Ludovic saved the firm from ruin, but all the same, we hate him for it because … well, because it makes us realise that Dad shouldn't have lost it.' Sara fidgeted a little, obviously finding it hard to explain. 'Dad couldn't help the way he was made,' she went on. 'I mean, we're all different. Dad had no sense of … well, he wasn't like Uncle Ludovic or Mother, they're crazy about the importance of money. Dad wasn't. Of course Granddad ran the business, but then he was ill and Dad took over and … well, the firm faced bankruptcy. Granddad didn't tell Dad or anyone, but he sent for Uncle Ludovic, who came down and started ordering everyone about, pushing Dad right out of everything.'

Jan listened silently, her eyes intent on Sara's face. Poor girl! How she had loved her father, and how she must have suffered for him. No wonder, Jan thought, it made Sara go to the other extreme and hate her uncle for what he was doing when in reality they should have been grateful.

'Dad and Mum kept quarrelling. It wasn't right of her, because he couldn't help being himself, could he, Jan? I mean, you're made like what you're born. You're either mad about making money or it doesn't mean a thing. It doesn't to me,' Sara said. 'Does it to you?'

'No. We need it to live on, but that's all,' Jan agreed.

'Of course Mum should never have married Dad. I think she was only interested in his money. She was hateful to him. I used to...' Sara jumped up and went to look at the grey rain-washed world outside the screened windows. 'I'm sure that's why he died, Jan. It just broke his heart. No one understood him except me and I couldn't do anything to help him.'

'You must have missed him terribly,' Jan said quietly.

Sara swung round, her face tragic.

'I had no one, Jan. No one at all to love me. That's why I'm ... I'm as I am. If only someone cared!'

'Your uncle does. He's very concerned.'

'Is he really? Or is it all talk?' Sara asked bitterly.

'And I'm sure your mother loves you.'

'Mother!' Sara's voice was bitter again. 'After Dad died, everything changed. She was never at home in the holidays, we hardly saw her. She's far too busy doing good in the world to think of us. She doesn't love us.'

Lucy appeared at that moment with the tea trolley and Jan was glad of the interruption, for what could she say? What was there to say? she wondered, as she let Sara pour out the tea and hand the little cakes to her.

'There's Jarvis…' Jan began.

'What does he care about anything but having a good time? Does your sister care for you?' Sara asked.

Jan frowned. 'I … I've always thought so, but … I don't know, Sara. Honestly.'

'Your mother loves you?'

'Yes, she's wonderful. She loves us, but we're free to do what we like. Within reason, of course,' Jan added, remembering Felicity's fury when their mother had insisted that Jan went with her to Australia.

'You're lucky,' Sara said.

'I know I am,' Jan agreed.

Esther came to join them.

'No, we've had tea, thanks. Barry wondered if you two would like to come and play canasta tonight?' Her eyes shone as she looked at Jan and nodded meaningly.

'I'd love to,' Jan said quickly. 'You'll come, Sara? Please?'

Sara shrugged. 'Sure. But Barry always wins.'

Jan laughed. 'This time we won't let him!'

It was much later that night, with the rain still thundering on the roof and the palm tree fronds drooping from the weight of water, that Barry, who had, as usual, won, looked at Sara.

'Your mother's rung up to say she's arriving tomorrow.'

'Oh no!' Sara sounded dismayed. 'She bringing that ghastly creature?'

Barry grinned. 'Of course. I wondered if you and Jan would like to come and meet them.'

'You know I never go to meet them,' Sara pouted.

He shrugged. 'I thought you might feel differently, seeing there's the two of you.'

'Do you think we ought to, Barry?' Jan asked, a little worried. After all, she was Mrs Fairlie's guest.

'There's no *ought* about it, but she's sure to be in a funny mood.'

'She hates it here, but has to put in an appearance now and then, as she's scared it may get sold if she doesn't,' Sara said quickly.

'Ludovic would never sell it,' Jan said firmly. 'He loves it.'

'He'll sell it one day – the day he goes back to his farm,' Barry replied.

Sara looked startled. 'Will he – ever?'

'You bet your sweet life he will,' said Barry.

'He's just waiting for young Jarvis to be ready to take over and then his uncle will be free.'

'I can't imagine him as a farmer,' Jan said.

How changed Barry was, calling her Jan, welcoming her to the Ryders' attractive flat, making her feel one of them, and she liked it, for it showed that Barry had accepted her.

'What do you think I should do, Barry?' Jan asked him.

He smiled. 'Want to make a good impression? I get it! I'd advise you to stay put, let her arrive, shower and rest and she'll be a different person. They're coming in the morning, round about eleven, so you two will be with Rab and can come up at lunchtime and meet her then.'

'Won't she think it rather rude of us?' Jan began, still worried.

'She won't think of us,' said Sara, jumping up and yawning. 'Well, I'm sorry you won as usual, Barry.'

'Male brains!' he said with a grin.

The three girls laughed scornfully and Sara, her head on one side like an inquisitive bird's, said:

'You're sure you don't cheat, Barry?'

'Sara!' Esther exclaimed, shocked, and Jan and Sara left in a cloud of laughter.

'I do like them so much,' Jan said as they went into their part of the big house.

'So do I,' Sara agreed. 'I don't know how I'd have stood it but for them.'

'You come here every holiday?'

'Of course. Where else is there to go?'

Another of Sara's unanswerable questions, Jan thought, as she got ready for bed. Sara's burst of confidence had opened her eyes to a lot of facts. She was seeing Ludovic's position with new eyes and she felt over-whelming sympathy for him, for whatever he did, it could be wrong to them. Ludovic had given up the life and work he loved to rescue the firm and the family money, and in return he was hated because he had done what Sara's father had failed to do. That wasn't Ludovic's fault, Jan thought indignantly. Yet she could see the other side of it, how it must have hurt Sara to have her father called a failure.

The next morning they went fossicking, but Jan noticed that Sara was much quieter than usual, and when she had a moment alone with Rab, she told him that Mrs Fairlie was arriving that morning.

'At long last,' Jan said, 'I'm going to meet my hostess.'

Rab gave her a strange look. 'Is she? I've

often wondered if she did invite you.'

Jan smiled. 'So did I wonder until her secretary...'

'Amanda Rowson?'

'Yes, she admitted that she had written the invitation.'

Amanda had also said that no dates had been given, but Jan decided not to mention this. It had puzzled her at the time. It still did. Could the answer be, she wondered, that Mrs Fairlie had left it to Ludovic to suggest an appropriate date?

'I thought from Sara's mood that something was wrong.'

'She says her mother doesn't love her, Rab.'

Rab sighed. 'You'll see for yourself.'

At the end of the morning they walked back slowly, almost reluctantly, as if dreading what lay ahead.

'It'll spoil everything, and we were having such fun,' Sara said as they came in sight of the long white house.

'We can still have fun,' Jan said, but without belief for she was wondering if Mrs Fairlie would have a talk with her, then politely say a formal farewell and suggest Barry took her to the mainland. After all, Jan told herself, she had been invited to the island merely to meet Mrs Fairlie, and once she had done that … well, the invitation was over.

The girls slipped in by a side entrance so that they could go to their rooms, shower and dress. They both came out at the same time and walked slowly to the verandah.

There was a sudden silence as Jan and Sara stood in the doorway. Jan immediately recognised Amanda Rowson, and thought she looked even more beautiful than before, in her sleek white trews and long blue and yellow embroidered white tunic.

'Oh, it's you,' said Amanda, her words ending on a flat unfriendly note.

'Sara, how nice to see you!' smiled the other woman.

Jan stared at Mrs Fairlie, for she wasn't sure what she had expected to see, but not this classically pretty face with its heavy make-up and carefully curled light brown hair and the long flowing, almost transparent, pale pink negligée.

'Hullo, Mother,' said Sara, and Mrs Fairlie's eyes passed on to Jan.

'You have a friend with you, Sara?' she asked. 'Do introduce us.'

Amanda spoke, her voice cold.

'She's your guest, Mrs Fairlie, Miss Janet Shaw.'

'My guest?' Mrs Fairlie's face looked puzzled. 'Did I … I mean, of course, I…' She looked at Amanda for help.

Amanda sighed heavily. 'You forget everything, Mrs Fairlie,' she said with a smile to cut out the acid note. 'You invited Miss Shaw to visit you as you wanted to discuss Jarvis's future.'

'Jarvis? What has Jarvis to do with…' Mrs Fairlie looked at Jan and smiled. 'Do forgive me, please, I'm notorious for my bad memory.'

'And that's no lie,' Sara muttered.

Her mother looked at her. 'What did you say, darling?'

'Nothing,' said Sara, going to sit down, tucking her legs underneath her.

Amanda sighed again. 'It was Ludovic's idea, Mrs Fairlie. He was concerned about Jarvis and said he thought a talk with Miss Shaw might help matters.'

'Really?' Poor embarrassed Mrs Fairlie was looking more puzzled than ever. 'Oh yes, of course.' She smiled at Jan. 'Do come and sit down and tell me how my son is. Up to his usual tricks, I suppose.' She looked up at Amanda. 'I think I would like to be alone with Miss Shaw.'

'Certainly. A pleasure,' said Amanda,

lifting her long cold drink and walking into the house.

Sara got up, but her mother waved her hand.

'You're Jarvis's sister, so you can stay. Amanda will interfere with my private affairs and it annoys me. This has nothing to do with her at all, so it's best we talk alone.'

She sipped her drink slowly and looked at Jan.

'Well, Miss Shaw, what have we to discuss?'

Jan laughed. She had not said a word yet, for somehow there had been no opportunity.

'Actually I don't know, except that I think your brother-in-law and you believe that Jarvis wants to marry me.'

'Jarvis? He wants to get married?' Mrs Fairlie sounded shocked for a moment. 'He's only twenty.' And then her face changed, brightened up as she smiled. 'But what a wonderful idea!' She looked at Jan. 'I take it you're English? Good. Better still. I'm all for mixed new blood into the country.'

Jan stared at her in amazement.

'You don't *mind* if Jarvis marries?'

'Of course not, my dear. Jarvis is old enough to know his own mind and it might

226

do him good. I think it would, responsibilities and becoming a father...' She paused. 'Oh dear, not too soon, I hope. I don't feel like a grandmother.'

'You certainly don't look like one,' Jan said, and had to laugh. 'I had an idea you'd already chosen Jarvis's future wife.'

'Chosen her? Good heavens, no! It's his life and he must learn by his own mistakes. Like we all have to.' A cloud of sadness seemed to cover her face. She bent forward and patted Jan's hand. 'My dear, just let the boy finish his Finals and then we'll discuss the wedding. Your mother will fly out from England, of course, but I'm sure she'd rather leave all the details to me to handle. I believe Amanda is very good at organising weddings and...'

Jan felt stunned. Everything seemed to have gone the wrong way, and she wondered how on earth she could get herself out of the mess.

'I didn't think you'd approve,' she said.

Sara was trying not to burst out laughing, one hand pressed against her mouth, as she rested her chin on her knees.

Mrs Fairlie smiled. 'My dear girl, I'm delighted. I'm sure it's what Jarvis needs – a strong-minded girl who loves him. Of course he's very young, but these days men do marry young. I suppose Ludovic doesn't approve?'

'I think he does,' Jan admitted.

'Tch … if only he would stop fussing! I believe in pushing your children out of the nest as soon as they can stand on their own feet. Don't I, Sara?'

Sara nodded silently. Jan wondered if Sara was longing to tell her mother that she had been pushed out too soon, that she would like to be in a nest where there was love and concern?

'Ludovic is a real old woman about some things,' Mrs Fairlie went on. 'He should marry, hurry up and have children and make them marry as soon as possible and then he'd be happy when they had children in turn. A real old patriarch, that's what he is, fussing all the time! We must make our own mistakes when we're young and pay for them.' She turned to Sara. 'I hear you were asked to leave school.' She laughed. 'Really, Sara, you do lead your poor uncle a dance. What is he going to do with you now?'

'I don't know. I haven't seen him yet.'

'You haven't seen him?' Mrs Fairlie sounded annoyed. 'Does that mean he'll be coming up soon?'

'He usually comes on Friday,' Jan told her.

'But that's tomorrow!' Mrs Fairlie sounded dismayed. 'Oh dear, I shall have to rush off again.' She stood up. 'Amanda!' she called, going into the house, calling again, 'Amanda!'

'Well!' said Sara, a smile splitting her face. 'You have landed yourself in a mess!'

'It won't hurt if they *think* it,' Jan pointed out. 'In the end, I'll tell your uncle the truth, or make Jarvis.'

Sara was giggling.

'You should have seen your face, Jan! You were flummoxed.'

'A very good word,' Jan had to laugh too, 'I felt it. Why must she rush away before your uncle comes?'

Stretching her arms, Sara laughed.

'To get Amanda away. You see, we all know Amanda wants to marry my uncle and none of us want her to as she is ... well, she wouldn't let him help us as he does. She's a greedy type. Mum knows this, so she does her best to keep them from meeting...'

She stopped speaking abruptly as the swing door opened and her mother stood there, looking angry.

'It is too bad – now Amanda isn't well. She's lying down and says she doesn't think she'd be fit to travel tomorrow and we have all those letters to write and phone calls to make. Really, it's most aggravating!' Mrs Fairlie sighed, then left them, swinging the door to again.

Sara chuckled, looking mischievously at Jan.

'Do you dig it? She's worried stiff about Amanda and about Uncle. You see the money's all tied up in a trust business and Uncle is the guardian and ... well, it'll be all right if he marries the right kind of person, but if not...' Suddenly Sara clapped her hands together, her eyes sparkling. 'Jan, I've just had a super idea. Why don't you marry Uncle?'

'Me?' Jan caught her breath. 'But why me?'

'Why not? You'd make a perfect wife for Uncle and I'd like you as an aunt.' Sara began to laugh. 'Don't look so horrified. I won't twist your arm!'

Fortunately at that moment there came the tinkle of the luncheon bell, so Jan jumped to her feet. Mrs Fairlie, like her brother-in-law, disliked unpunctuality.

'Seriously, Jan, think about it,' Sara said, slowly rising. 'It's just an idea.'

A crazy idea, Jan thought. Unfortunately she thought about it all the time.

Jan had often wondered what sort of woman Mrs Fairlie would prove to be, and had rather dreaded meeting her, expecting Jarvis's mother to be as critical of her as Ludovic obviously was. However, to Jan's surprise they got on well. Mrs Fairlie could be charming, and, to Jan's amazement she seemed to want to be on good terms and was willing to talk.

'I find it a most engrossing and satisfying life, doing what little I can to help such poor tormented creatures as kangaroos, who are being shot all the time. Ludovic, of course, doesn't agree with me,' Mrs Fairlie said, as later, after lunch and a siesta, she joined Jan and Sara on the veranda. 'He says they're vermin. I can't agree.' She flashed a smile at Jan and glanced at Sara, who was staring out at the lagoon, her face stiff. 'I hope I'm not boring you?' Mrs Fairlie went on.

'Most certainly not,' Jan told her with genuine eagerness. 'Anything about Australia fascinates me.'

'Dear child!' Mrs Fairlie's voice had a faint tinge of patronage, but her smile was friendly. 'How sweet of you, and so sensible. When you marry a man of another nationality it's wise to give up your own and assume his.'

'In England we think of Australians as our cousins,' Jan said quickly.

Mrs Fairlie smiled again.

'A nice thought. Would you care to see my scrap books?' she asked. When Jan nodded, Mrs Fairlie turned to Sara. 'Would you get them for me, Sara? They're in the bottom drawer of the desk in my room.'

Sara uncurled herself from the cane chair and went into the house, her long pale blue trousers and matching tunic suiting her.

Mrs Fairlie sighed as she looked at Jan.

'Such a difficult age, my dear. I'm so glad you're here with Sara, she needs someone of her own age.'

Jan flushed. 'I'm nineteen, Mrs Fairlie.'

'Is that so? You girls look so young today. Ah, here we are!' Mrs Fairlie said as Sara came back with two big black-covered books.

Jan had not lied when she said she was interested in everything to do with Australia. It was not only because of Ludovic that she found it a fascinating, exciting country, but its size amazed her, and the progress it was making. Now as they went through the album of photographs, in every one of which Mrs Fairlie stood, looking elegant and charming, Jan saw a real cross-section of Australia from the lovely harbour of Sydney to the fascinating Alice Springs country.

After dinner, Mrs Fairlie listened to the radio as a speech she had made was on and Sara and Jan slipped away. Sara went into Jan's room and sat on the bed.

'Isn't she a bore?' Sara sighed.

'No, she isn't,' Jan said, and smiled. 'I suppose you're heard it all so often.'

'You're so right. I could recite it all backwards.' Sara jumped up and began to walk restlessly round the room. 'How she loves an audience!'

Jan sat down on the window seat. 'Don't we all?' she asked quietly.

Sara stood before the mirror, looking at her reflection, turning sideways, moving backwards, and then she laughed.

'Touchée, Jan. We're all as bad as Mother, but sometimes it gets me down.'

'I'm sure it does,' Jan said gently.

A knock came on the door.

'Come in!' Jan called.

It was Esther. They had not seen her since Mrs Fairlie and Amanda arrived. Now she smiled and came in, closing the door behind her and leaning against it.

'Barry's going to show the slides,' she laughed as Sara groaned, 'and Mrs Fairlie thought Jan would be interested.'

'Of course. Slides of what?' asked Jan, jumping up and smoothing her white dress down.

'Slides of Mother's trips round the world,' Sara said moodily. 'I might have known it. She never misses out on a newcomer.'

'By the way, how's Amanda?' Jan asked as she ran a comb through her hair, which she let fall to her shoulders, a cloud of black beauty.

Esther smiled.

'She's eating well but still in bed. She seems quite happy, but I guarantee she'll have recovered by tomorrow afternoon when...'

'Uncle comes,' Sara finished the sentence for her. 'So do I. Mother's mad as can be with her.'

'Let's face it,' said Esther, 'Amanda does work very hard for your mother, so perhaps she really is ill.'

'Not likely! Mother heard Uncle was coming up, so she rushed off to tell Amanda they must leave the next day. I bet Amanda felt ill then and not before. She's determined to see Uncle and Mother's lost this time,' Sara chuckled. 'What a game!'

Was it a game? Jan thought miserably. If it was, then it was a game in which her heart was involved.

'Well,' Esther's hand was on the door knob as she prepared to go, 'the slides will be ready in ten minutes.'

'See you there?' Jan asked.

'In the background,' Esther smiled. 'Safest place when...'

'Mother's about,' Sara finished as Esther left the room. 'Mother likes to throw her weight around, Jan. Sometimes I wonder if she suffers from hallucinations and thinks she's a duchess or something. Barry resents it, and I don't blame him, for he and Uncle went to school together and have been close friends all their lives. You can go if you feel you should, but tell her I've got a headache – if she asks where I am,' she added bitterly.

'Of course she will,' Jan said quickly.

But Mrs Fairlie didn't.

'Come in, Janet, and sit by my side so I can explain everything.'

There was a big white screen on one wall, Barry standing behind the projector in front of it. It was an interesting collection of slides and Mrs Fairlie seemed to enjoy telling Jan just where they were taken and why. In most of them Mrs Fairlie appeared.

''Amanda is a good photographer,' Mrs Fairlie said. 'I taught her.'

Some of the slides had pictures of Ludovic. These Jan longed to ask to be shown again. None of them had Sara or Jarvis in, she noted, with a heavy heart.

That night Jan found it hard to sleep. It was a hot night and she kept thinking of what Mrs Fairlie had said as they parted to go to bed.

'My brother-in-law is coming tomorrow and I'll speak to him, Janet. I'm sure marriage to you would be the answer to Jarvis's problems. He's an adult now and should be treated as such. I'll do my best to make Ludovic understand, but I can promise nothing, because he can be difficult and unfortunately Jarvis is his ward until the boy is twenty-five. My father-in-law was strict and old-fashioned in his views, I'm afraid, and made a very difficult and unfair will,' she said.

'So now what about tomorrow?' Jan asked herself. How would Ludovic react? Would he accept Mrs Fairlie's advice and tell Jan she had better return to Sydney, to be by Jarvis's side? Or would he advise her to stay where she was until the Final exams were over? Mrs Fairlie was talking about making arrangements for the wedding. She had suggested having it in perhaps four or five months' time. Jan had not known what to answer, for she seemed to be getting more and more involved every moment. She could be honest, of course, and tell them that a mistake had been made and it was Felicity that Jarvis loved ... but then Ludovic might be annoyed with Jarvis and all this be for nothing.

But then Jan knew it could never be *for nothing* – she had not only had the most wonderful holiday, made friends such as Esther, Sara and Barry, but had the chance to know and love a wonderful man like Ludovic. She drew a long deep breath and told herself that although she knew she was heading once again for heartbreak yet there had been much happiness, too.

In the morning Jan and Sara went fossicking as usual. Mrs Fairlie said she had letters to dictate, for she could use Ludovic's dictaphone and Amanda could type the letters as soon as she was well.

It was a perfect day, as every day in this paradise seemed perfect in some way or another, Jan thought as they followed Rab as he balanced precariously on the coral reef, searching for some special specimen. But that evening, Jan reminded herself, Ludovic would come, and what would happen then? Would he refuse to listen to Mrs Fairlie? Or would he change his mind and agree that it would be a good thing if Jan married Jarvis?

After a shower and a change into more formal clothing, Jan and Sara had tea on the verandah with Mrs Fairlie, who said she had slept well that afternoon.

'It's really rather pleasant to be on one's own sometimes,' she said, and from the quick look Sara gave Jan, she knew that Mrs Fairlie was thinking of Amanda, the beautiful, brilliant and efficient secretary who could, apparently, be rather a trial at times.

They were startled when they heard the clatter of horses' hooves and watched the carriage come to a stop outside the house. They watched silently as Ludovic got out and turned and helped ... Amanda out.

Jan heard Mrs Fairlie give a quickly suppressed gasp of annoyance.

'I thought...' she began, then stopped and waited, her eyes cold.

Ludovic walked slowly, Amanda, beautiful in a jade green suit, holding his arm, laughing as she looked at him.

'Hullo, Agnes,' Ludovic said to his sister-in-law, and smiled at the others.

Amanda, by his side, also smiled.

'I thought it would be nice if someone met him.'

'I thought you were too ill to work,' Mrs Fairlie said stiffly.

'I was,' Amanda agreed, going to sit by her employer, giving her a sweet smile. 'I felt fine after lunch, though, and thought the fresh air might help me. You were sound asleep and I thought it better not to disturb you.' She smiled again. 'I know how much you enjoy your afternoon siesta, so I asked Barry to take me. I feel much better now.'

Amanda smiled at Ludovic and he smiled back. It made Jan catch her breath. A real pain gripped her for a moment as she closed her eyes.

A fear that she had felt before now became a truth. Ludovic loved Amanda. A smile like that could surely only mean ... Jan thought miserably.

She slipped away quietly as Ludovic sat down, talking to his sister-in-law. Alone, Jan stood very still. How could she bear it? The answer was simple. She had no choice.

CHAPTER SEVEN

In the morning there was no sign of Ludovic. It was Saturday, so Rab wouldn't be coming, and Sara and Jan, meeting on the verandah, decided to go for a swim and then sunbathe. They could hear Amanda's deft fingers flying over the typewriter keys as she coped with the work that was waiting for her. There was no sign of Mrs Fairlie, either.

'Where's your uncle?' Jan asked, as casually as she could as they settled on the hot sand.

'I don't know.' Sara, in a minute scarlet bikini, stretched her arms and legs luxuriously. 'I bet he's gone off fishing with Barry. Anything to get away from four women!' she added with a laugh.

'He seemed to be enjoying himself last night,' Jan pointed out, remembering the previous evening miserably. 'Sara, are you sure he's *not* in love with Amanda?' she heard herself ask, then wondered if it was wise, but it was too late, for Sara rolled over, turning her head to stare at her.

'What makes you think he is?'

'Well...' Jan searched for the right words. 'Well, she went to meet him and ... well, he was holding her arm as they came in...'

'No, Jan, *she* was holding his,' corrected Sara, beginning to smile. 'Go on.'

'Well, last night, for instance. He sat by her, he even danced with her.'

'Again she made the move, Jan. Didn't you hear her say she felt like dancing? I mean, it could have been either of us, for Uncle's crazy about dancing and will always fall for that line.' Sara chuckled. 'She looked like a cat that's just swallowed cream, didn't she?'

'Then you do think...?' Jan hesitated, afraid of giving away the truth, that she was insanely jealous when she saw someone else in Ludovic's arms.

'No, I don't.' Sara rolled over on her back, resting her head on her arms. 'I can't somehow see Uncle marrying her.'

'But he does seem to like her. I mean...'

Sara laughed. 'Oh, Jan, you are dumb! He does that to make Mother mad. You see, Uncle Ludovic has a weird sense of humour, he loves teasing people, making them feel and look fools.'

'That's for sure!' Jan agreed fervently. 'And he certainly succeeds.'

241

'That's where you're all so stupid,' said Sara, sitting up and hugging her knees, turning to look at Jan who was lying on her back, her black cloud of hair spread over the towel laid on the sand. 'So long as he knows he's made you feel a fool he'll go on playing tricks. He's given up trying with me, 'cos I never let him see it hurts.'

'But why should liking Amanda anger your mother?' Jan began, then nodded. 'I remember, you're afraid the wrong kind of wife will influence Ludovic as regards your allowances, but isn't it all legally decided?'

Sara laughed.

'Of course, but actually, you know, Uncle is very generous and gives us more than we need. My mother is afraid, though, that if he's married, his wife may not approve.'

Jan sat up suddenly, hugging her knees, too, turning to look at Sara and only vaguely seeing the lovely background that normally she would be admiring.

'Do you *honestly* think Ludovic would let any woman influence him?'

Sara shrugged. 'Men are strange, sometimes. If he was handled diplomatically – well, maybe. She might say it wasn't good for us, that we should stand on our own feet, perhaps she could convince him.'

'That's a thought,' Jan agreed, nodding slowly. 'You know Ailsa? I told her, I think, that she turned up. She found me here and was furious, tried to throw me out. She called me a trespasser.'

'I bet she was mad,' Sara laughed. 'Any competition terrifies Ailsa. She lives in a dream world, because Uncle would never look at her.'

'She's very lovely.'

'Her looks are all right, but...' Sara lifted a handful of sand and let it trickle through her fingers.

'But?'

'Well,' Sara laughed, 'Ailsa is a name-dropper and a social climber – these are two things my uncle can't stand. Neither can I, for that matter.'

'A name-dropper? I don't get it.'

Sara laughed. 'Honestly, Jan sometimes I feel years older than you! You just don't seem to know anything. A name-dropper is one who would never say she'd stayed in Lisbon but would always say at the Hilton hotel in Lisbon, or at the Ritz in London. Also she goes out of her way to meet important people and is always talking about my dear friend, Lord Gough or Lady Catherine, we were at school together. Maybe they were, but who cares? Get me?'

'Yes, I do.'

Jan lay down again, wishing she could be sure Sara was right about Ailsa and Amanda. All the same, Jan thought, she could not forget the way Amanda had smiled at Ludovic, and Ludovic had smiled back.

Jan and Sara had a pleasant morning, moving down to the lagoon where they floated peacefully, then later ended it by lying in the shade of a huge palm tree.

'This place really does have something, doesn't it, Jan?' Sara asked, her voice sleepy. 'I always feel so happy here. I almost like Uncle.' She rolled over to look at Jan. 'Can you?'

Jan stiffened as the unexpected question frightened her, for it would be so easy to give the truth away. Sara was remarkably quick about discerning things and if she knew, what would Sara do? Would she see it as a great joke and tell Ludovic? He would laugh, Jan thought unhappily, and how humiliated she would be.

So Jan told a truth that was no longer true.

'I don't think I've ever hated a man so much,' she said, hoping Sara would not notice that it was the *past* tense she was using.

Sara yawned. 'That goes for me, too.'

They dozed and were surprised when they awoke and saw the time. They strolled back to the house, chatting happily, and Jan was totally unprepared for what awaited her.

Lunch was ready and they were late after they had hurriedly showered and changed into clean shorts and shirts. Mrs Fairlie and Amanda were sitting at the table and, to Jan's complete surprise, Ludovic was there. He turned as they entered the room and as soon as she saw the look in his eyes, her whole body tensed in preparation for what might lie ahead.

'Late as usual,' Ludovic said cheerfully. 'Sit down and let's eat this delicious meal. I must say Esther is a very capable house-keeper.'

It was a good meal, lobster and salad, followed by chocolate mousse, but it might have been sawdust for all Jan noticed. However, as the meal came to an end they were all talking about various subjects, some of her tension left her so that when, as they drank coffee, Ludovic leaned forward, looked down the table to where she was sitting, and addressed her, she was totally unprepared.

'Jan,' he began, 'I'm glad to tell you that

my sister-in-law and I have reconsidered the situation of you and Jarvis.'

Jan's mouth was suddenly dry. She looked wildly down the table and Jarvis's mother smiled triumphantly. Amanda looked bored, and Sara's eyes were wide open as if she, too, was surprised by Ludovic's words.

'As you know,' he went on, 'we both felt Jarvis was too young to consider marriage, but his mother has made me change my mind.'

Ludovic smiled at Jan, who stared back, as if hypnotised. She had been afraid of this, yet had felt comfortingly sure he would not agree with Mrs Fairlie.

'You see, Jan,' Ludovic leaned back and made a little steeple with his fingers, 'you're quite different from the kind of girl Jarvis usually falls in love with, and since you've been with us, we've come to know and like you. So...'

There was an utter silence, a silence that could be felt as they all looked at him. Jan hardly breathed; she could not believe this was happening.

'So we're going to allow him to marry you,' Ludovic finished. He leaned forward. 'Now you will be happy, won't you?' he asked, with a smile.

Jan stared at him helplessly. It couldn't be happening, she thought, it couldn't be true! And then she saw his smile and she was suddenly sure that Ludovic had discovered the truth about Jarvis and Felicity and this was his idea of a joke. He knew she didn't love Jarvis, nor Jarvis her.

'I think it's a splendid idea,' Mrs Fairlie put in. 'Amanda, you must look up my itinerary so we can choose a date I'm free.'

Jan turned to her. 'I can't help wondering if we shouldn't wait a few years. Three or even four, perhaps...'

Ludovic laughed. Jan glared, for she knew he was enjoying this.

'Three or four years,' Ludovic echoed, his voice sarcastic. 'I can't see Jarvis agreeing to that.' He stood up. 'That reminds me, Jan, I've cabled your mother and invited her out to the wedding. Personally I think next month would be a good time. I've also contacted Jarvis, who is coming up here as fast as he can.' Ludovic smiled at Jan. 'You look surprised.'

She drew a long deep breath; she must keep her temper.

'I am surprised,' she admitted. 'After all, you made it very plain you didn't approve of the idea, before.'

247

'Ah, that's where I erred,' said Ludovic, leaning on the table and looking at her with that hateful smile round his mouth. 'You see, I didn't know you then. Now, if you'll all excuse me, I have some phone calls to make.' He turned to his sister-in-law. 'Don't worry about a thing, Agnes. Leave it to me. We'll have the wedding here and give a really good reception. Sara and Jan might start drawing up a list of guests. I imagine it will be in the hundreds, but that doesn't matter. Jarvis doesn't get married every day.'

He smiled at them and left the room. There was a long silence and then Mrs Fairlie began to stand up and so did Jan, quickly and quietly, so that she left the room first. She hurried to her room, still stunned by the whole thing. Why had Ludovic behaved like that?

As she passed his door, it opened and he came out, saw her and moved rapidly to her side.

'Well, satisfied?' he asked, smiling down at her. 'You won. I never thought you would – did you?'

Before she could speak, he caught hold of her, pulling her close to him, bending and kissing her. It was a long lingering kiss and she closed her eyes, afraid lest he see the expression in them. If only the kiss could go on for ever, she thought miserably, if only ... but then he moved away and she stood, a little unsteady, putting out her hand to feel the wall, as she stared up at him.

'Don't look so horrified,' Ludovic told her with a smile. 'After all, in a little while I shall be your uncle-in-law.'

He was laughing as he walked away.

CHAPTER EIGHT

Jan dreaded the weekend ahead, for it would have a nightmarish quality, but if she got through Saturday and Sunday somehow, on Monday Ludovic would fly back to Sydney. For once, she knew, she would be glad.

On Saturday Ludovic and Amanda went out in the cruiser. Jan was left with Mrs Fairlie and they sat on the verandah while Mrs Fairlie complained as she read through her letters. Sara had vanished, but Jan knew she wasn't with Ludovic and Amanda, which made thinking about them worse than ever.

'Really,' Mrs Fairlie was grumbling as Jan listened vaguely, too wrapped up in her thoughts to really understand what was being said, 'actually it's Ludovic's fault. He's so inconsiderate and can't realise how important my work is.'

Jan made an effort to be polite and said, 'You've got more lectures to give?'

Mrs Fairlie looked shocked.

'Of course. They never stop. I talk at Book

Club luncheons too. It's the only way to get all those poor creatures helped by making people know just what dreadful things are happening.'

Jan tried to listen and to reply intelligently, but her thoughts were with those on the cruiser as she wondered if Ludovic was taking Amanda in his arms ... if she had linked her hands round his neck as she pulled his head down closer ... closer... Perhaps they were even planning their marriage, Jan thought unhappily. Despite what Sara had said, Jan couldn't help feeling that Ludovic found Amanda both beautiful and interesting.

On the Sunday they all went out in the big cruiser. Mrs Fairlie looking elegant in her white trouser suit, her hair beautifully done, but her face bored.

'I could hardly refuse Ludovic's invitation,' she told Jan quietly as they sat together. 'After all, I am his guest.'

Jan glanced along the deck and saw Amanda standing by Ludovic's side. She was laughing at something he had said and Jan thought she had never seen her look so beautiful.

Jan's eyes smarting, she looked at the long slow rollers of the beautiful sea, and told herself she had no right to be jealous, no right at all. Ludovic had not spoken to her since he had kissed her, not a word since he had been so horribly pompous and reminded her that he would be her uncle-in-law.

What was he playing at? she asked herself, twisting her fingers together, listening vaguely to what Mrs Fairlie was saying. Why was Ludovic forcing her to marry Jarvis? Or perhaps it would be better to say, appear to be going to marry Jarvis? And Jarvis? When he came to the island, the whole thing would be cleared up and all would be well. But would it?

'...of course he does like being the big noise...' Mrs Fairlie was saying, and Jan came back to the present. 'Not that I really mind, of course, because he will pay the bill.'

'He will?' Jan said, for Mrs Fairlie was looking at her and obviously expecting an answer.

Mrs Fairlie nodded.

'He has so many friends, so the wedding will be a real social event. I'll certainly fly up to be here, of course. I must say, it's a great weight off my mind, because I really haven't time to organise the reception.'

Jan listened silently. So Sara was right; her

mother loved neither of her children. How tragic it was, she thought, remembering her own mother and the deep love they had for one another. Love was infinitely more worthwhile than all the money in the world. Mrs Fairlie wanted to have nothing to do with Jarvis's wedding, it was too much trouble, or perhaps not enough publicity? Jan thought, then felt ashamed, for once, years before, she could remember her mother explaining why one of Jan's school friends had a mother who had deserted her.

'All women aren't *born* mothers, Jan darling,' Jan's mother had told her. 'Some have no love for their children. The tragedy is that so often they are the ones who have babies, while those with real love in their hearts don't have children at all. But don't blame the mother too much, Jan darling. You can't *make* love when it isn't there.'

Sunday night came at last and in the morning when she awoke, Ludovic would have gone, leaving Mrs Fairlie and Amanda behind, for they were not leaving until the Monday afternoon.

Jan lay, straight and stiff, in bed, as she remembered the little scene she had witnessed unintentionally. Amanda had suggested a walk in the warm moonlit night and Ludovic had stood up at once, looking at them all.

'Coming,' he had said, but in a most un-inviting voice, his eyes daring Jan to accept the invitation. She was tempted to jump up and say she'd love to … but the way Ludovic turned his head and smiled at Amanda stopped her.

'Lazy lot!' he said, giving them no time to accept or refuse and, taking Amanda's arm, he led the way out into the garden.

Mrs Fairlie was reading and hadn't looked up. Sara was sprawled on the carpet, yawning as she played with a jigsaw puzzle, an unusual habit of hers, but she had told Jan privately that it was the only way to keep her mother from telling her the boring news of her latest lecture.

'I've heard it so often, Jan, it drives me round the bend. Mother must have an audience, regardless of whether they're interested or not. This jigsaw puzzle makes her shut up.' She laughed. 'Or at least, turn to someone else!'

After Amanda and Ludovic had gone, something had made Jan jump up.

'I've got a headache,' she said, and it was partly true, only she should have said *heartache*. 'Goodnight.'

Sara looked up with a smile, ''Night,' but Mrs Fairlie was lost in the book she was reading and didn't hear a thing.

Jan went to her bedroom and, without thinking, out on to the wide verandah that ran all round the house. She stood there, leaning on the white rail, the light in the bedroom behind silhouetting her, as she looked at the lovely lagoon where the moon shone and the tall palm trees moved slowly in the slight breeze. It was then that she saw them. They were standing on the sand by the gentle lagoon water, too far away for Jan to see their faces, but she saw Amanda turn to Ludovic and put her hands round his neck, and Ludovic bend his head as he took her in his arms.

Jan turned quickly, running into her bedroom, closing the windows, jerking the curtains across and standing still, her hands pressed against her face.

So she was right. And Sara was wrong, she thought. Ludovic *was* in love with Amanda.

Somehow she had undressed and managed to tumble into bed, where she lay very still.

Tomorrow he would have gone ... but only for five days, and then he would be back, looking at her with those amused eyes. And

Amanda? Perhaps they arranged to meet when Amanda had time off. According to Mrs Fairlie, she demanded far too much! With money and private planes, it would be easy enough for Ludovic to see Amanda frequently, and without Mrs Fairlie knowing anything about it, Jan thought unhappily.

But surely Ludovic, if he loved Amanda, wouldn't waste his time deliberately involving Jan in an embarrassing situation? Yet that was what he was doing, Jan knew. She was sure that Ludovic had discovered about Felicity and was angry with Jan and Jarvis for deliberately deceiving him, so was punishing them by putting them in a humiliating position, and humiliating, Ludovic would make it, Jan was sure of that.

The door quietly opened.

'Asleep? Sara asked.

Not sure she wanted the interruption of her thoughts, Jan sat up, her cloud of black hair falling behind her pale unhappy face, as Sara came in and closed the door, sitting on the bed, her feet curled under her.

Chuckling, Sara said:

'They've come back, Amanda looking mad as hell. I wondered what Ludovic said to her.'

'Amanda mad?' Jan repeated slowly.

'But…' She stopped, for she couldn't tell Sara what she had seen. After all, it might look as if she had been snooping, but if she had, it was subconsciously.

Sara nodded.

'She stormed off to bed. Perhaps she wanted to stay out in the romantic moonlight longer.' She laughed. 'She'll never hook him, Jan, don't worry.'

Jan caught her breath. She stared at Sara, her eyes widening with dismay.

Sara laughed, but it was an affectionate, not a cruel laugh.

'Jan, it stood out a mile, right from the beginning. You're crazy about him, aren't you?'

'I … I…' Jan's mouth felt dry. 'I…'

'Don't worry, Jan, I'd never tell him,' Sara promised, and Jan relaxed.

'He must never know,' she said anxiously.

'That's why you're so worked up about the wedding, is it?' Sara asked, twisting her body into a more comfortable position. 'What's Ludovic's idea?'

Jan moved her hands expressively.

'I think he's angry with Jarvis and me for pretending that we're in love so as to keep him from knowing about Felicity.'

'What's wrong with Felicity?' Sara asked.

'I mean, if Ludovic...' Jan noticed that Sara no longer spoke of her *uncle* but called him by his Christian name, and she wondered why. But this was no moment to ask her.

'I might have been wrong, but Felicity is only seventeen, and if Ludovic thought *I* was too young at nineteen and Jarvis at twenty, then he'd really take off about a seventeen-year-old. Then Felicity is quite different from me. She's a professional dancer and loves it. I doubt if she'd ever give it up, because she dreams of being a famous film star one day...' Jan paused. 'Somehow I can't see Ludovic approving of that.'

'So!' Sara rested her chin on her drawn-up knees. 'So you reckon Ludovic is mad at you and Jarvis? Right? Right. And you think he's baiting you about this so-called wedding and will make you feel small. Right?'

Jan nodded miserably.

'Right. When Jarvis comes, it'll be different. We'll tell Ludovic that it was all a ... well, a...'

'You were only trying to protect Jarvis and Felicity,' Sara finished for her. 'Very commendable.' She chuckled. 'See what talking to you is doing to me, Jan? I'm using long words!'

'What have I to do with that?'

258

Sara rocked herself as she laughed.

'Everything! Ludovic feels you've been a good influence. He congratulated me to-night on the change in my behaviour. He said I was acting like an adult and not a spoilt child. You're educating me, Jan, and helping me to become a lady...'

Jan began to laugh and felt better for it.

'That's absurd!'

'Jan, to return. You love Ludovic, don't you?'

Jan stared at her. 'I'm afraid so.'

Sara had stopped laughing. 'I'm afraid you haven't a hope,' she said slowly. 'He respects you, likes you, I think, but ... love? That's different, isn't it?'

'Very different,' Jan said miserably. 'Ah well, when Jarvis comes, it'll all be cleared up and then I'll go.'

'You'll go?' Sara sounded shocked. 'But why?'

'What else can I do? I can't stay here for ever. I ... I think I'll fly back to England.'

'Do you think Ludovic is really sending your mother a cable?'

Jan shook her head.

'I don't. If he is, I'll stop her coming. I'm writing to her tomorrow and I'll tell her the whole story.'

'What will she say?'

Jan smiled.

'She'll understand. Probably say it was foolish of me, but she'll be sympathetic.'

Sara jumped up and yawned.

'I'll be on my way. Don't worry, Jan, I promise I won't tell anyone.'

'Thanks, Sara,' Jan said, and when the door was closed, she closed her eyes, too, for at least she had a friend now to whom she could talk. Sara would always understand.

The next morning the house bustled with action, for Mrs Fairlie was going to leave that afternoon and her clothes had to be pressed, her papers gathered together, and Jan and Sara hurriedly got out of the way and joined Rab. Later they lunched with Mrs Fairlie and Amanda and bade them farewell.

'Next time I see you will be at the wedding, Janet,' Mrs Fairlie said with a smile.

'If you remember,' Amanda murmured.

Mrs Fairlie looked at her sharply.

'I don't have to remember. That's what I pay you for.'

Jan saw the quick colour in Amanda's cheeks and wondered why she tolerated such bad temper on her employer's part. But now Amanda was smiling.

'I know, and I earn every penny I get, don't I?' she said laughing.

Mrs Fairlie laughed too. 'And that's no lie!'

They were both laughing as they got into the carriage and the black horses trotted off.

Sara whistled softly. 'Thanks be, now we can relax and enjoy ourselves. Let's go and get Esther and take her for a swim.'

'Mind if I don't?' Jan asked. 'I want to write to my mother.'

Lifting her eyebrows, Sara looked solemn. 'Project Important, right?'

'Right,' Jan laughed. 'I think I'll feel happier when I've told her everything.'

Jan wrote a long letter, sitting alone on the quiet verandah. She began from the day she arrived in Australia.

'It wasn't easy finding somewhere we could afford. Rents are very high. It was rather a scruffy flat, but we could see the Bridge if we leant out of the window, and Kings Cross is the "with it" part of Sydney. Jarvis was very helpful and found me a good job.'

She went on writing, telling her mother about George who was handsome and smooth.

'I felt very proud when he sought me out

and the other girls were jealous, and then...'

Oddly enough, she thought as she wrote, she could think of George without regret or pain, indeed all she felt was a sense of anger at her own foolishness; the way she had jumped to conclusions that weren't there, in fact, as Ludovic would have said, the childishness of her behaviour.

'Felicity and Jarvis were sweet to me, Mum,' Jan wrote, 'and when Felicity went north for this dancing job – actually she was hoping to get something on T.V. as a result – Jarvis took me out and helped me. Then suddenly this man turned up, Ludovic Fairlie.'

This man. Jan stared at the words. *This man* – what a way to describe anyone like Ludovic, she thought.

'He's a sort of business tycoon, frightfully rich and bossy, arrogant and can be very unkind. Likes to make you feel stupid, if you know what I mean, Mum.'

It wasn't as hard as Jan had expected to tell her mother the rest of it – the invitation, the realisation that Jarvis must have let his uncle believe it was Jan he loved, for some reason.

'I think Jarvis's uncle would have thought Felicity too young, just as you did, Mum. I felt I must help Jarvis, for he'd been so sympathetic. Also I wanted to get away from Sydney. I couldn't bear to be near George – then, I mean. So the invitation for a holiday came at the right moment.'

Jan wrote about her surprise when she found herself on the island and of the non-arrival of Mrs Fairlie, then the rows with Ludovic and his moral blackmail.

'You see what kind of a man Ludovic is,' Jan wrote. 'He said it was up to me. I could help Jarvis or hurt him. I ask you! So I stayed on. Then Jarvis's mother did come and I was sure she would be against it, but to my horror, she wasn't. When Ludovic came, he said he'd changed his mind and I'm to marry Jarvis, and the wedding is being arranged...'

Jan stopped writing and read the words back. It sounded rather hysterical, but she had felt like that at the time.

'Actually, I'm not worrying now, Mum, because Jarvis is coming up and we'll tell Ludovic the truth – though, actually, I think he already knows it's Felicity Jarvis loves and Ludovic is doing all this just to humiliate me, but when we tell him, there'll be a big row and then I'm coming back to England. Oh, by the way, Ludovic said he was sending a cable to you to come out to the wedding. Don't come, Mum, there isn't going to be one.'

Jan signed the letter, folded it and put it in an envelope and stamped it. She wished she had written it earlier and then Barry could have posted it on the mainland after he had seen Mrs Fairlie and Amanda off in the plane. However, he was sure to go in tomorrow or the next day and there was a whole month ahead and air mail would get the letter back in plenty of time.

Oddly enough when Barry returned that night, there was a letter from Jan's mother in the post.

Jan read it eagerly.

'I've just heard from Felicity, Jan darling, and in case she hadn't written to you, and knowing our Felicity, I doubt if she *has* written, this is to let you know Felicity is back in Sydney and is sharing your flat with your friend Iris. Felicity is thrilled as she is being auditioned for a T.V. job and she says Jarvis agrees that she must work at her career at this stage. It sounds as though they're still very much in love.'

Jan took a long deep breath. That was good news! She had had a vague uncomfortable feeling that Felicity might have changed her mind about Jarvis and that he might not be feeling very fond of the Shaw sisters!

'Felicity envies you your lovely holiday,' Jan read on, 'and wishes she had been around when the invitation came as it sounds terrific. But it does seem to me, darling, that you've been there for rather a long time and might be outstaying your welcome. It's kind of the Fairlies, but you mustn't impose on them, even though you are so happy there. Also don't forget how easy it is for your shorthand speed to drop when you're not practising.'

Jan folded the letter and put it in her writing case. Well, her own letter should answer her mother's question. Jan would soon be leaving the island and on her way back to England – and home.

Home. This island had become home, the only home she wanted, with Ludovic there, Jan thought, and buried her face in her hands. That was a dream that could never come true.

CHAPTER NINE

Jan's letter lay on the hall table until Wednesday. Not that it really worried her because it had not yet been posted, as there was plenty of time. The house seemed quiet with the weekend visitors gone, but Sara seemed far more relaxed and kept including Esther in their afternoons and evenings.

'No good moping, Jan,' Sara said on Tuesday evening. 'You have to learn to live with it – or so they say.'

Jan had to smile. 'Hark at Gran talking!'

'You learn a lot at boarding school, you know. Jan, I have an idea I have a crush on Rab.'

'He's a darling, but…'

Sara was sprawled on the sheepskin rug in the lounge, listening to the latest pop tunes.

'*But*… I know. Don't worry, I'm going to see the world and sow my wild oats before I settle down and marry. Do you think I'd make a good model, Jan?' She jumped up, walking round the room with mincing steps and laughing.

'Frankly,' Jan said; she was also laughing.

'No,' Sara agreed. 'Well, Ludovic and I were talking before he left, when he congratulated me on growing up – I told you about that, didn't I? He asked me if I had any ambitions and I said just to have fun and he thought it a good idea, but he said I'd need a job or something as a girl with my intelligence would be bored to tears, with nothing to do. Think he's right, Jan?'

Jan nodded.

'I think so, but it depends where you are. I could stay here, doing nothing, and not be bored.'

'Ah!' Sara laughed. She lay down on the rug again. 'But that's different. The island means much more to you than just an island. It's Ludovic's home.'

'I suppose so,' Jan sighed. 'Have you any idea what work you'd like to do?'

'I'm thinking about it, very seriously. You see, I'm good at languages. Maybe I could be a courier, an air hostess or something. Anyhow, Ludovic asked me if I'd like to go to a college or something in Paris. I ask you, Jan. Wouldn't that be thrilling?'

The door opened and Barry stood there.

'I've just heard from the master,' Barry said; he was in one of his formal moods.

'He's coming up tomorrow, so I wondered if you wished to come with me to meet him.'

Sara sat up. 'Don't think so, thanks, Barry. But perhaps you would, Jan?' She turned to Jan, her eyes amused. Just like her uncle's, Jan thought.

She shook her head. 'No, thanks. Why's he coming back again so soon? He only went the other day.'

Barry shrugged. 'The master doesn't have to explain his actions.'

'Barry, shut up about the master. How about you and Esther coming and listening to my new records?' Sara asked.

He pulled a wry face. 'That tripe? No, thanks!'

'Barry,' Jan said quickly, 'You won't forget to take my letter tomorrow? It's important.'

Barry stiffened. 'I never forget letters,' he said, and left the room.

Sara laughed. 'You've hurt his feelings, Jan.'

'I didn't mean to, but it is an important letter.'

'I know.'

'I wonder what time Ludovic's coming,' Jan mused.

'Late afternoon, I expect, as he usually does,' Sara told her.

But it was early afternoon this time, for

the next day they fossicked with Rab in the morning and had only just finished lunch and gone out to the balcony for coffee when they heard the clatter of hooves and the carriage appeared.

'Who's he bringing with him?' Sara asked, leaning forward to try and see.

Jan's heart seemed to skip a beat. It could only be Amanda! But it wasn't. It was Jarvis.

She stood up as Jarvis came towards the house. The moment of truth had come sooner than she had expected. Ludovic followed him, with his briefcase, a smile playing round his mouth. Jarvis pushed open the swinging door.

'Hi,' he said, looking at his sister and then at Jan. At that moment Ludovic followed him on to the verandah.

'Jan, isn't it wonderful?' grinned Jarvis, striding towards her and putting his arms round her and kissing her.

She moved away quickly. 'Wonderful?'

He caught hold of her hand and swung it gently.

'Yes, I mean about the wedding. We never thought they'd agree, did we?'

She stared at him. Was he trying to tell her that he wanted her to go on playing the game, as obviously it was not the moment

269

for confession?

'No, we didn't,' she said, trying to quietly release her hand, but his fingers held it firmly.

Ludovic spoke for the first time.

'I'm sure you two have a lot to discuss. Why not take her for a walk along the lagoon, Jarvis?'

'Super idea, Uncle.' Jarvis turned and grinned. 'Come on, Jan, we've so much to talk about.'

There was nothing she could do; in fact, she wanted to be alone with him in order to get the whole matter settled, so she went.

Jarvis pulled her so fast down the slope to the lagoon that she was breathless by the time they got there. She glanced up, but they couldn't be seen from the house, as a group of palms stood in the way. This was not where Ludovic and Amanda had stood, that night when he had kissed her, Jan thought.

'Why are you looking so shocked, Jan?' Jarvis asked, sitting on the sand, pulling her down by his side.

'Not shocked, puzzled. How long must this farce go on, Jarvis?'

'Farce?' he frowned. 'I don't dig it.'

'I mean, this pretending that you love me

and want me to marry you...'

'What do you mean, pretending?' Jarvis asked.

Jan turned round, startled. 'But we are pretending.'

He looked at her, and he wasn't smiling.

'Who said we were pretending?'

'Jarvis, are you out of your mind? There was never anything between us.'

'Wasn't there? Yet you came up here to meet my mother?'

'But ... but look, Jarvis, I knew you wanted me to pretend because you thought they'd disapprove of Felicity.' Jan's voice rose.

'Who told you that?' Jarvis frowned. 'I don't understand. You mean all the time you've been up here, it was to...'

'Help you, Jarvis. Felicity is so young, only seventeen, so I knew if Ludovic – your uncle, I mean – disapproved of me for my age group, I knew he'd be even more against Felicity. I thought that was why you'd told your mother you loved me.'

'You thought...! No one *told* you!'

'Jarvis, please.' Jan was getting flustered. 'Look, you and Felicity fell in love in England, you asked her to come out here so you could both decide if it was serious. I've just heard from Mum, she says Felicity is back

271

in Sydney and you both seem even more in love than ever.'

'Seem,' he said. 'And don't forget Felicity sent the letter.'

Jan stared at him in real dismay.

'But you can't... I mean, you don't ... you couldn't... I mean...'

'Just what do you mean?'

His cold voice reminded her still more of Ludovic. Jarvis could only be joking, she told herself, for he was teasing her, like his uncle.

'You love Felicity.'

'Do I? Shouldn't I be the one to know that?'

'But, Jarvis...' She leant back against her hands, feeling exhausted.

He knelt and turned to look at her.

'You listen for a change. What reason is there to stop me from loving you? You're quite a dish.' He smiled, 'You're brainy, far wittier than Felicity. You're more mature, for one thing. For another, what about her ambitious future? Think a husband can fit in with that? Surely, Jan, there's no reason why such a marriage as ours shouldn't be a success? Responsibility will make a man out of me, as Uncle pointed out, somewhat belatedly.' Jarvis smiled for a moment. 'We're fond of one another. You are, aren't you?'

She stared at him.

'I am. I do like you, but … Jarvis, that isn't love. It wouldn't work.'

'It might – if there was no other man. There isn't, is there?'

He startled her, seizing her by the shoulders and staring closely into her face.

She forced herself to stare back at him, hoping her eyes wouldn't betray her.

'Of course not, Jarvis. Who could there be?' she asked.

'Then I see no reason why the wedding shouldn't go on. Love often comes after wedding bells have rung.'

'I don't see how it can,' Jan said desperately.

He let her go and stood up.

'Well, let's forget it for a while and just have fun. I need a holiday after all my hard work.' He pulled her to her feet.

'But, Jarvis, we must tell Ludovic.'

'We can't do that.'

'But we must,' Jan insisted.

Jarvis looked at her. 'All right, if you insist.'

She felt suddenly limp with relief.

'Thank you, Jarvis. I know it won't be easy, for either of us, but…'

'We'd better go up to the house, then,' he

said, and led the way, his shoulders hunched, his face sad.

It worried her, so she hurried to catch him up and slipped her hand through his arm.

'Jarvis, please, you don't really love me, do you?'

He stared at her. 'Don't I?' he asked. 'You seem to know best.'

He walked away, hurrying to the house, as if as eager as she was to clear up the mess they had got in.

But *was* he telling the truth? she wondered. Had she been an absolute fool all the time?

Sara was on the verandah. She greeted them with a grin.

'Well, Jarvis, I never expected this of you!'

Jarvis smiled ruefully. 'It's amazing what a delectable dolly can do for a man. Where's Uncle?'

'Oh, he's gone,' Sara said casually, picking up the magazine she had been reading.

Jan leant against the door.

'Gone? Already? But...'

Sara picked up an apple from the bowl on the table.

'Yes, you'd just run off when a phone call came through. Something urgent has happened, so Barry's rushing him back to the mainland. Luckily Uncle has his own plane, so he's not dependent.'

Jan sank into one of the chairs. She was conscious that she was both disappointed and relieved. She had not been looking forward to the moment of confrontation with Ludovic – yet at the same time, the longer it was postponed, the harder it would be to do.

Jarvis vanished into the house and Sara looked at Jan.

'Neither of you look very happy,' she said, her eyes twinkling.

'Oh, Sara, it isn't funny. I just don't know what to think.'

'Then ask Gran's advice. What happened?'

Jan told her. 'I can't believe it's me he loves,' she finished.

Sara whistled softly. 'That really is a spanner in the works, Jan. Think Jarvis means it?'

'I don't see how he can. We were only friends. He was kind to me.'

'That doesn't sound like Jarvis.'

'Well,' Jan said, 'I'm Felicity's sister and I was sure…'

'*You* were sure?'

'Oh, that's what Jarvis said. What a mess I've got us into!'

'But you said your mother had a letter from Felicity saying they were more than ever in love?'

Jan shook her head.

'I didn't actually say that. Mum wrote "*it sounds as though they're very much in love.*"'

'But she's only got Felicity's side of it, Jan.'

'That's what Jarvis said. Oh, Sara, I can't bear it if I have to hurt Jarvis. He wants the wedding to go on. He said you often loved people after the wedding bells had rung.'

'I wonder what book he's been reading, Jan. Yet in a way I suppose it's true. Look at the countries where marriages are arranged. People seem happy enough.'

'Seem being the objective word,' Jan said bitterly. 'It wouldn't work. Jarvis and I aren't right for one another.'

Sara leaned forward, her voice soft.

'Are you sure? Isn't that just because you love Ludovic? You know you haven't a hope there, so why not marry Jarvis and try to find happiness?'

Jan stared at her in horror. 'Marry Jarvis just because I...'

'Need someone to love. That's what you need, Jan, make no mistake. I think you could be happy together and I'd love you for a sister-in-law.'

'But that's daft!' Jan stood up and went to the door, staring at but not seeing the island's beauty. 'I couldn't, Sara. I just couldn't!'

Sara sighed. 'Ah, well, you're the one involved. It's just tough on poor Jarvis. I suppose we'd better behave as if nothing's happened, as we can't do anything until Ludovic comes back.'

Jan swung round. 'And then?'

Sara looked at her.

'You'll have to tell him.'

'I know,' Jan said, and escaped to her usual sanctuary, her bedroom. There she sat, staring into space, as she tried to sort out her confused thoughts.

Had she led Jarvis to believe that she loved him? she asked herself first. She was sure she hadn't, she tried to comfort herself by deciding. Then there was the chance that he wasn't telling the truth, that he was doing a Ludovic-trick, to make her feel and look a fool. Or could it be a sort of red herring or shield that Jarvis was using, she wondered, planning to elope later with Felicity and defying his uncle? Yet if that was so, surely he could have confided in Felicity's sister?

She stood up wearily. She couldn't answer the questions, so it was a waste of time to brood. She'd have a shower, she decided, and as soon as Ludovic returned, she would tell him the truth.

CHAPTER TEN

Of course it was easy enough to make a decision, but sometimes impossible to carry it out, and in this case, Jan's trouble was that Ludovic made no reappearance. She couldn't understand it as Friday passed and there was not even a message from Ludovic. He had not phoned Barry, yet never before had he missed coming on a Friday.

'I wonder where he is,' Jan said, without thinking.

Jarvis glanced at her.

'With his girl-friend, I expect.'

'Amanda?' Jan asked.

He shrugged. 'Could be. He has quite a harem, has my handsome uncle.'

They were having dinner and Jan thought how fortunate it was that in this awkward situation Jarvis was being so helpful, for he had done what he suggested, postponed all discussion of the wedding and, like her, she imagined, was waiting for Ludovic to appear.

Jarvis treated her as he had always done, ever since the day Felicity had met him in

Lewes and brought him home. Friendly, always joking, planning a game or outing, he and Sara got on remarkably well for a brother and sister, Jan thought. Jarvis also insisted that the Ryders join in and share the fun. Sometimes they danced, or played canasta, but not once did he say anything to Jan about their future, and finally she cornered him.

'Jarvis, I *must* talk to you,' she said.

She felt she had to straighten something that worried her. They were alone on the verandah. He looked at her. He was very unlike his uncle, she thought. Tall, thin, wearing modern gear, as he called it, tight blue cotton jeans, with a yellow shirt and a white cravat tied round his neck. His hair was cut short and his eyes wary as he stared at her.

'So what?'

'What about Felicity?' Jan asked. 'Is this fair to her?'

'Is what fair?' He sat up, a half-smile appearing round his mouth.

'Well, all this...' Jan waved her hand vaguely. 'I know she's in Sydney. Does she know you're up here?'

'Of course. I told her.'

'She didn't mind?'

Remembering Felicity's jealousy, and couldn't understand it.

Jarvis shrugged.

'Why should she?'

'But ... oh, Jarvis, she loves you.'

'Does she?' He sounded disinterested and stood up. 'I thought we agreed to forget the whole thing until my uncle gets here. He'll settle everything.'

Jan stood up, too, her cheeks suddenly hot.

'What do you mean?'

'Look,' Jarvis spoke very patiently, 'my uncle is the "Master of Barracuda Isle". You agree? Well, what he says goes. If he says the wedding must go on, it'll have to.'

'It will not!' Jan said angrily. 'I'll not be bullied into a marriage that can only ruin our lives.'

'But why should it ruin our lives?' Jarvis asked quietly. 'Uncle Ludovic is always right and what he decides, I'll agree with.'

'He can't make us...' Jan turned away, so angry she found it hard to speak. 'After all, he's only a man. He has no right to rule our lives, to be a dictator and lay down laws. I'll tell him so.'

Jarvis laughed. 'I should. He'll enjoy it.'

Her tears were perilously near as she

glared at him.

'Are all Australians like you two? You treat us girls as if we don't matter. So long as you're the bosses, that's all you care.'

'Of course it is.' Jarvis sounded surprised. 'Isn't that what a man is for?'

He opened the door to the garden and left her alone. She sat down as the anger swept through her. *Isn't that what a man is for?* Jarvis had said. Wasn't that exactly the way Ludovic always behaved? Well, she was one woman who was not going to lie down meekly and obey him! She...

She tried to calm herself down, for the anger wouldn't get her anywhere at all. There was no real problem, she told herself sternly, and pulled the vase of lovely jasmine-scented white flowers towards her. No problem. All she had to do was to tell Ludovic the truth, apologise and explain that Jarvis must have misunderstood and then she would go. It was as simple as that.

She was sure Ludovic was only waiting for such a showdown, but he was determined to humiliate her so that he was putting on the pressure to make her feel trapped.

Ludovic's macabre sense of humour might even make him continue with this farce right to the altar in order to make her lose face and have to admit what an idiot she had been. That was all he wanted. To – as the Australians called it – cut her down to size.

Yet how could the Ludovic she loved, be so mean and so cruel? It didn't make sense. But then nothing on this lovely island, so green with its beautiful bushes, so bright in colour with its lovely flowers, so serene, so... She swallowed. It was so beautiful, yet nothing seemed to make sense here.

On Sunday morning, Jarvis decided to go fishing with Barry.

'No message from Uncle, so Barry is free. How about coming?' Jarvis asked the girls.

Sara thought it a wonderful idea, but Jan excused herself out of it, pleading a squeamish feeling that the sea was too rough.

'Don't be chicken,' Jarvis teased, but Sara took Jan's side.

'It's ghastly being seasick, so I don't blame you, Jan. See you later.'

Jan waved them goodbye and sat alone on the verandah, pretending to read. But she could not concentrate. Why hadn't Ludovic come up the day before? she kept asking herself. Maybe he was ill, she thought worriedly, or was he deliberately leaving her in this awkward situation to put the pressure on still harder?

How quiet everything was. She noticed as she looked round that everything reminded her of Ludovic. She could not forget him, but how was she going to bear what lay ahead of her when she left the island for ever?

Suddenly she knew she could not just sit there, so she changed into white shorts and a yellow shirt, and went outside. The lagoon by the house was very still, the huge waves breaking against the reef on the other side. It was no fun to stay there alone, for she was thinking too much. Thinking, that got her nowhere, she knew that! So she decided to walk through to the other lagoon. She could wait there for Sara and Jarvis to return and might even find some shells for Rab. Of course, as it was Sunday he wouldn't be there. However, she walked on, taking the beauty of the small birds for granted, not giving the sleeping flying foxes a glance, for she could think of one thing alone and the words sounded in her head with the awful regularity of a clock ticking.

If only ... if only ... if only ... if only.

A stupid thing to think, she told herself, but the words went on and on: *If only ... if only...*

And then she saw Rab. He was wearing a

thin cotton suit and standing by the small jetty, not fossicking for once. She shouted and waved and he came hurrying towards her.

'I thought you wouldn't be here,' Jan said as he reached her.

'I shouldn't be normally,' Rab said. Somehow he looked different, Jan thought, and the way he was staring at her puzzled her. 'I had to come,' Rab went on. 'I was so worried about you.'

'Worried – about me?' Jan was startled.

'Look,' he said, taking hold of her arms with his gentle fingers. 'Is it true?'

'Is what true?'

'That you're going to marry Jarvis?'

'Who told you... I mean...' Jan began.

Rab stopped her.

'Amanda Rowson told me. Is it true, Jan?' He paused and went on, 'If it is, you mustn't. Jarvis isn't ready for marriage, and certainly not to a wonderful girl like you.'

Jan stared at him, amazed. Rab was not the type of man to hand out compliments.

'I'm not going to marry Jarvis,' she said.

His hands fell away and he wiped his face with the back of his hand.

'Thanks be,' he said gravely. 'Why did Amanda say you were?'

'Oh, Rab, it's a long story and I was such a … a fool,' Jan confessed, her voice unsteady.

'Let's sit down, then, and you get it off your chest.'

Rab took hold of her arm and led her to a dry rock. They sat with their backs to the water. Jan sighed. Everyone would know eventually, so she might as well tell him… So she told him everything and Rab listened silently. When she had finished he looked surprised.

'Somehow I can't imagine Ludovic behaving like that. It doesn't make sense.'

'Nothing does – here.'

He turned to look at her. 'I thought you were looking pretty miserable yesterday, but I had no idea … look, aren't you making a mountain out of a molehill, Jan? I mean, Ludovic can't *make* you marry Jarvis.'

'I know. I'm going to tell him so. It isn't only that…' She turned away, her eyes smarting.

'Jan.' Suddenly Rab's arms were round her and he was pulling her close to him, just as Peter Frost, Ludovic's friend, had done, but very differently. Rab's movements were tender. 'Jan,' he said, looking down at her as she lay across his knees, 'I love you. I love you so much. I would have told you before, but I thought you were Ludovic's girl.'

She looked up at him and his face seemed blurred as the tears gathered in her eyes.

'I am.'

Rab frowned. 'But then why is he playing this trick on you?'

'Because ... because he's got a strange sense of humour. He doesn't see me as *his* girl; as a girl, I don't exist to him. It's just that ... that...'

Suddenly she was crying. Rab rocked her to and fro gently, stroking her soft dark hair.

'My poor little Jan,' he said, and there was sorrow in his voice, real pain. It helped to stop the tears.

'I'm sorry, Rab,' she said, and he helped her sit up, gave her a handful of tissues to wipe away the tears. 'I'm most terribly sorry, Rab,' Jan said when she had recovered composure. 'I had no idea.'

He smiled ruefully.

'Just my bad luck. You met him first. If you hadn't...'

Jan looked at Rab's kind face, remembered the happy hours they'd spent together, also how often she had thought how much she enjoyed being with Rab, how restful it was. She smiled at him.

'Perhaps, Rab. I like you so much.'

'I'm afraid that's not enough.' He stood up, pulling her to her feet gently. 'Look, Jan, promise me you won't marry Jarvis? Only unhappiness for you both could result. You will tell Ludovic everything?'

'Of course.'

'And what will happen then?' he asked as they walked slowly across the sand and the woods. As they talked, she thought she heard the sound of the cruiser, but didn't turn round as she was in no mood to meet Jarvis and Sara. If she didn't see them she needn't stop, she knew.

'I'll go back to England, Rab.'

'I see. You live at … where is it? Lewes? Know something, Jan? You're going to be pretty miserable. I'm going home next month too. Let's go back together. You can meet my folk, I can meet yours. We'll just be friends, Jan. I won't rush you. But perhaps, in time, your liking for me might change.'

'Rab, you're so sweet,' Jan turned impulsively to him. 'I'd like us to be friends, but…'

He smiled. 'I won't expect more than friendship, I promise.'

Walking back towards the long white house, they talked of the future. Rab came from Penzance. He said he had been out there for several years writing a thesis, selling articles as a help. Now it was finished and he was eager to get back to England.

'This is a lovely spot,' he said, 'but give me England every time.'

Jan moved automatically by his side. How her mother would like Rab. Maybe he was right; maybe if they were just friends, in time she would forget Ludovic and...

They had just come out of woods when the carriage with the two black horses trotting gracefully along passed them. Ludovic was in it. He stared at them. With him was another person, but Jan could not see her face. Could it be Amanda? she wondered.

Rab's arm was round Jan's shoulder, her face tear-stained, her hair untidy, and then the other person in the carriage, stood up and Jan saw who it was.

'Mum!' she shouted as the carriage rolled by. 'It's my mother!' she called to Rab as she ran down the road. What was she doing there? Had Ludovic gone so far as to cable her as he had said? How could her mother afford the fare for what was going to be a nothing?

But her joy at seeing her mother made her run fast. Rab fell behind, not attempting to keep up.

The carriage stopped and Ludovic helped

out his companion. How young her mother looked, Jan thought, as she came closer. No one would think she was in her late forties, with that lovely smoky-blue hair, beautifully waved under the absurd but attractive wisp of a lacy hat, blue to match the well-cut suit.

'Mum!' Jan shouted, nearly falling over herself as she got closer.

'Darling!' exclaimed her mother, holding wide her arms to hug Jan. 'Darling, it's lovely to see you!'

'Oh, Mum, Mum!' Jan hugged her. There was so much to say.

'I've arranged that the room next to yours is for your mother, Jan,' Ludovic said, his voice calm, his eyes narrowed as he looked down the road at Rab, standing there, watching them. 'I suggest she has a shower and a rest.'

'I didn't see you come in,' Jan said, still hugging her mother. 'We were by the lagoon.'

'I saw you,' said Ludovic, his voice cold now. 'You were too engrossed to notice us.'

Jan felt her cheeks burning. Just how much had Ludovic seen? Had he seen her in Rab's arms, seen him dry her tears? Or only seen them walking along, Rab's arm lightly round her shoulders?

'Come with me, Mum,' she said, and led the way to the house.

In the bedroom, very similar to Jan's but with a different colour scheme, a warm apricot-pink, her mother smiled.

'I must say it's hot,' she said, looking round. 'A lovely room.'

'Everything here is lovely,' Jan said eagerly. 'Don't you think so?'

'It is.' Her mother smiled at her. 'Why were you crying?'

Jan felt herself blushing.

'Well, you see, Rab, the man I was with – well, he wants to marry me.'

'Ludovic invited me for the wedding, but I thought it was Felicity and Jarvis. He said nothing about *you* getting married.' Her mother looked puzzled. 'Look, I think I'll have a shower and then we can talk.'

'You didn't get my letter?'

'Which one?' her mother asked as she quickly undressed.

'The last one,' Jan said, then realised that the remark was of no help at all. 'I told you all about Jarvis.'

'Jarvis? No. Have you found out something about him you don't like?' Her mother sounded worried.

'No, it wasn't that, Mum. Have your

shower and then I'll tell you,' Jan promised.

Jan perched on the bathroom stool while her mother showered, then curled up on the bed as her mother unpacked and put on a jade green housecoat. She talked of the flight out and of her surprise when Ludovic walked into the boutique with the news.

'Not that I was really surprised, darling,' Jan's mother said as she carefully combed her hair and patted it. 'Your letters gave me a clue. You obviously made a good impression on Jarvis's mother.'

'Did I?' said Jan.

'I must say he's a remarkable man... Ludovic, I mean.' Jan's mother went on, leaning closer to the mirror to powder her face. Looking in the mirror she could see her daughter.

'He's ... he's certainly remarkable,' Jan agreed. 'I don't think I've ever hated any man so much,' she went on. 'He's ruthless, harsh, arrogant, domineering...'

'And adorable,' her mother said softly.

Jan swung round. 'What did you say?'

'I said adorable.' Her mother came to sit on the edge of the bed and smiled. 'You're hopelessly in love with him, Jan, aren't you?' she said gently.

Jan turned her head away quickly.

'I hate him!'

She felt her mother's hand on hers, warm and loving.

'Jan, sometimes love is strange – it can be born out of hatred, cherished by hatred, and do you know why? Because one uses hatred as a defence. When you love someone and you know it's hopeless you pretend to hate to protect yourself and you say that you wouldn't marry him if he was the last man in the world. You're afraid to admit the truth. Why else could you hate him? Do you know that your letters were *full* of Ludovic? Yet you hate him. Why?'

'Because he's...' Jan drew a long deep breath. 'I wrote to you, Mum, and told you everything. The letter you didn't get, I mean. I told you I wasn't going to marry Jarvis.'

'I got no letter – and what has Jarvis to do with you?' Her mother looked surprised. 'Jarvis and Felicity are in love, so I understood.'

'So did I ... it's a long story, Mum.'

'Then I'll sit on something more comfortable, Jan.' Her mother said, moving to the armchair near the open window, opening her handbag and lighting a cigarette. 'You still don't smoke? Lucky girl. I keep giving it up, but I'm afraid I'm a weak character. Well now, how does Jarvis come into all this?'

'Didn't ... didn't Ludovic tell you that I was going to marry Jarvis?' Jan began.

'No. He merely invited me out here for a visit. He said there was going to be a wedding in the family. I took it for granted it was Felicity and Jarvis, of course. It's been one mad rush, so really we had no time to talk.'

Jan began to walk round the room.

'Look, Mum, it all began when I was washing my hair and Ludovic arrived...'

Her mother listened and then at the end stubbed out her cigarette and smiled.

'Problem easily solved, darling. Just tell Ludovic the truth and everything'll be all right.'

'But I love him and ... and he'll just tear me to bits,' Jan said desperately.

Her mother stood up and patted her hand.

'Do you think he will? I wonder.'

'The difficulty is to get him alone...' Jan began, and stopped talking when she saw her mother smiling. 'All right,' she agreed, 'I admit I'm dreading it.'

'But why, darling? The worst he can do is...'

'Make me squirm and feel ashamed of myself. I know! I only wanted to help Jarvis and now I've got involved. If only Jarvis would tell the truth – I know he doesn't love me or want to marry me. It's all so...'

'Look, Jan, go along and see Ludovic now while I rest. The sooner you get it done the better. You'll feel much happier, darling.'

Reluctantly Jan obeyed. The door to Ludovic's study, which was a small room next to his bedroom, stood open. Jan hesitated in the doorway. Ludovic, who was writing at the desk, looked up.

'Could I speak to you?' she began, her hands damp with nervousness.

He was on his feet.

'Of course. Actually I was going to ask you to come along and see me, but I thought you'd have a lot to say to your mother first. What a charming woman she is, Jan. So amusing too.'

'Ludovic, I want to tell you.'

'Sit down. What about a cold drink, Jan? It really is hot, today. I was afraid your mother would find it too much, but she seemed to enjoy it...'

Ludovic was talking as he went to the small bar in the corner with its little fridge, took out the ice and made them both cool lemon drinks. He sat down facing her and smiled.

'Well, we're a happy family now, aren't we?'

'Ludovic, I want to…' Jan began again, but Ludovic wasn't listening. He leant forward.

'I was telling your mother how much I owed you, Jan. Somehow you've opened my eyes and I realise what a lot of mistakes I've made. Maybe it's my age – but somehow I didn't see anything in the right perspective. You made me see that I can't help Jarvis by denying him responsibility. I can see that Jarvis will be helped most by being allowed to marry the girl he loves. You see, Jan, what a help you've been? Mind if I smoke?'

As she shook her head, he leant back in his chair, slowly packing his pipe, smiling at her.

She sat very still, slightly dazed by it all, trying to sort out things but only becoming more confused.

'I've even told Jarvis that if he really hates working in the family firm, we'll find a solution. In any case, I'm planning to resign and go back to my…'

'Farming?' Jan was startled.

He smiled.

'Why not? Certainly I prefer to call myself a grazier rather than a farmer, but it means the same. Don't I look like a … what you'd call a farmer?'

She stared at him; at his bleached fair hair,

his strong face with the amused eyes and mouth that was obviously trying not to laugh at her. She clutched the arms of the chair she was sitting in, for she longed to tell him the truth; that, no matter what he looked like, she would still love him.

'By the way,' Ludovic abruptly, 'what was it you wanted to see me about?'

A chill seemed to spread through her. She shivered and then stiffened, drawing a deep breath, for the moment had come.

'I'm not going to marry Jarvis.'

'I know,' he said. She stared at him. Then he continued: 'Judging from the way you lay in Rab's arms, might I ask if he is to be the lucky man?'

Jan winced. Why had Ludovic to be so scathing?

'Rab was comforting me because I was upset,' she said angrily. 'He also asked me to marry him.'

'Did he now? And what was your answer?'

She clenched her hands into fists, trying to control her anger.

'I don't love him, so I told him so.'

'I see,' Ludovic said slowly, almost as if he was interviewing an employee, she thought angrily. 'You don't love Rab, you don't love Jarvis, then who do you love?'

Jan caught her breath. She couldn't speak. Her body ached with the desire to tell him the truth – to yell the word *you* at him. Her hands even itched to grab something and throw it at him. How could he be so...

'I see you prefer not to answer my question,' Ludovic said gravely, then she saw the twinkle in his eye.

'You know,' she said accusingly, standing up, leaning over the desk. 'You always have known, haven't you? You thought it a great game, making me look a fool!'

Ludovic smiled.

'Of course I knew. What *you* don't know is why I invited you here. Please sit down, I hate females who lean over my desk and look as though they're about to scream hysterically at any moment.'

Jan flushed, backed away, fumbled with her hand to find the chair and finally sat down.

'Why did you invite me here?'

He leaned forward. 'Because I wanted to get to know you.'

She stared; suddenly something in her mind seemed to click.

'We had met, then...'

'We hadn't *met,*' Ludovic corrected her gravely, 'but we had seen one another. You were dancing with Jarvis at the University Ball. You looked terribly unhappy and I wondered why. I asked Jarvis and he told me the whole story – of Frank and George and your desire to get away from Sydney with its memories. I already knew all about Felicity and actually I was the one who got her the job in Cairns. I thought it might be an idea for her to be away while Jarvis studied.'

He spoke calmly, almost impersonally, and Jan sat very still, trying to grasp it all. So she *had* seen him before, she thought. At the time she had felt sure. His was not the sort of face you forget.

'And that, my dear Jan,' Ludovic went on, using his patronising voice, 'is why I invited you up here. I was interested in you. You seemed a staid sort of girl, rather an unusual type to be so romantic-minded. I knew you needed a holiday, so...'

'You got your sister-in-law to write the invitation?'

'I knew that was the only way I could get you.' He smiled. 'Was it such a crime?'

'You knew all the time...' Jan began, and Ludovic moved fast, jumping up, going round the desk, as she said, 'I hate you! I hate you!'

He caught hold of her hands and pulled

her to her feet, then smiled down at her.

'No, you don't, Jan. You love me, don't you?'

Her eyes were wide with dismay, her mouth quivering as she stared at him.

'How did you know?'

'I knew the day I kissed you. When I was fool enough to introduce you to Peter. I'm cynical, Jan, I was afraid you *might* be interested in my money. I didn't know you so well, then. You didn't like his brash approach, so I tried mine. I knew then that you loved me. Did you?'

Silently Jan nodded. He knew it all, now. She waited for his hands to drop hers, for that sarcastic patronising smile to return, to hear his advice on how not to be so stupid.

But instead he smiled.

'I knew I loved you – that first time I saw you at the Ball.'

She gasped. It couldn't be true ... she must have imagined the words, she thought.

'You mean? B-b-b-but you can't,' she stammered.

'But I can – and do.'

As he spoke, he linked his hands behind her back and pulled her closer, so that she had to lean against him, bending her head back to look into his face.

'But … but…' She felt dazed.

'But I do,' he repeated, and bent his head, gently kissing her.

It was a long satisfying kiss. When he released her, her cheeks were red, her mouth quivering.

'But – but if you loved me, why were you making me marry Jarvis?'

He laughed. 'I wasn't. Jarvis *is* going to marry Felicity and you're going to marry me. We'll have a double wedding.'

Jan shook her head, trying to clear the muddled thoughts and straighten everything out.

'I don't understand. Why did Jarvis pretend?'

'Because I asked him to, Jan. You see, I knew you'd been badly hurt and hated all men. Somehow I had to break down the barrier and make you see men as not *all* hateful. I also had to anger you, bring you back to life, because you were going through a very emotional phase and I knew I hadn't a hope unless I could get you out of it. A different emotion is the best cure, so I made you hate me. It worked, didn't it?' He smiled at her. 'I got Jarvis and Felicity to help me. If you had examined Jarvis's words, you would see he never once said he loved *you* – you believed he meant that, but he only implied it.'

'Did you bribe them?' she asked, then wished she hadn't, but Ludovic only laughed.

'I used what you'd call moral blackmail, I guess, but I call it a new way of looking at things and a new approach to the difficult young. Jarvis is free to do what he likes with his life and I shall increase their allowances. Sara likes you and is thrilled at the thought of going to Paris. So all is well. They like you and I like Felicity. Any complaints?'

Suddenly she found herself clinging to him, her arms locked round his neck. She began to cry.

'Now what's wrong?' he asked, pretending to sound exasperated. 'Can't I do anything right?'

'I just can't believe it,' Jan whispered, her mouth close to his. 'I just can't believe it, but whatever you do is right.'

He chuckled.

'I hope you remember that all our married life, Jan.'

He kissed her and said very softly, 'Have I told you lately that I love you?'

The publishers hope that this book has given you enjoyable reading. Large Print Books are especially designed to be as easy to see and hold as possible. If you wish a complete list of our books please ask at your local library or write directly to:

Dales Large Print Books
Magna House, Long Preston,
Skipton, North Yorkshire.
BD23 4ND